D1566666

WHITE FLUTTERS IN MUNICH
an E.T. Madigan mystery

Joan Wright Mularz

ISBN-13: 978-1518871603

ISBN-10: 1518871607

PART I

Simple white leaflets fluttering to the
ground
Their effect profound

Good people feeling fluttering in their
gut
Yearning to help, but

Most went white with fear of retaliation
The silent nation

Rare few showed courage

Chapter 1 — *Haus* Schumann

Vroooom! The cars seem hell-bent and rocket-fueled! Our own speedometer reads 120 kilometers and the contents of my stomach keep threatening to gurgle up through my throat. It's not so much our speed that's bothering me but the motion sickness I get looking at the other cars whizzing past us.

A few kilometers back, we crossed the border into Germany, our home for the coming year. So far, the landscape seems clean and neat and I wonder what it will be like for me, Ellen Madigan. As an archeologist's daughter, I'm used to adjusting to new places. I've liked some better than others but even my least favorites have been interesting, especially the archeological digs. This one will be different though, because Dad won't be working outside. Instead, he'll be an advisor at a museum in Munich for a special exhibition.

I'm on the German Autobahn with him, my mom Carolina, and my brother. (His name is Alexander but I call him T.G.) The only one missing is my sister Cat. We delivered her to the American University of Paris yesterday for her first semester.

****

We're off the highway and in city traffic now and Dad says we're getting close to our rental. We pass through a busy square, enter a quiet street, and stop in front of a plain stucco house.

Dad says that we're to get the key from *Herr* Hofstetter. He's the owner of the house at number 28 next door and he's expecting us.

Aware of his sketchy German skills, Dad squares his shoulders and takes a deep breath before he leads us to number 28. As he rings the doorbell, I check out the place. It has trimmed flowering bushes that have been recently watered and a freshly swept walkway and steps. The brass handle on the wooden doorway is polished and gleaming and a small window on the door is backed with starched white lace curtains. Spotless… everything is spotless. It's obvious that kids don't live here.

Wrong! The door opens and we're facing two kids — a girl of four or five and a *fine* looking boy about my age. Before Dad can speak, the boy says, "Hallo! You will be Mr. Madigan. I will tell Papa you are here."

While we wait, my eyes are drawn to a small metal sign cemented into the wall of the house. It says *Haus Schumann, gebaut 1952*. I can't understand the German words but I get the strange feeling that it's trying to tell me something, and a shiver runs up my spine.

Herr Hofstetter, unlike his son, greets us in German and gives us a warm *Wilkommen*. He is a tall man with big hands. He shakes Dad's hand, points to himself saying, *"Ich bin Franz Hofstetter"* and then motions for us to enter.

The kids are waiting for us in the living room with a small woman dressed in brown pressed pants and a beige sweater. The totally cute boy introduces her as his *mama, Frau* Silke Hofstetter. Silke… such a smooth sounding name… especially the way this boy says it.

Frau Silke points to her son and daughter, calling them Sebastian and Annika. Sebastian shakes hands with Dad and Mom and then Mom, who always learns a few words of a language before we get to a place, bends down and says, "Annika, how old are you… vie alt?" The little girl shows five fingers. Then Mom stands up and says, "Sebastian, you must be close to Ellen's age. She's fourteen. Am I right?"

Sooo embarrassing!

He says he's fifteen and then he *smiles* at me and I feel the heat rising in my cheeks.

I'm grateful when *Frau* Silke says something and leads us into another room. Here a silver-haired older lady wearing an apron over a polo shirt and workout pants introduces herself to us in English. She is *Frau* Silke's mother, *Frau Doktor* Sabine Müller. Sebastian calls her *Oma* and explains that it means *grandma.* His grandma immediately apologizes for her casual clothing explaining that she has just returned by bicycle from a clinic where she volunteers. I'm just thinking that I've never seen a doctor in an apron before but I don't say it. Instead, I ask where she learned such good English.

Tipping her head to one side causes her short, straight hair to bounce as she says, "At university, but you are very kind, Ellen. My English many years ago when I was at hospital was very good but now not so much."

"Well it's way better than my non-existent German words!"

She laughs and says, "You see. Already I don't understand all of your words! Come now and please, everyone, sit down."

The cloth-covered table is set with small plates. Noticing the surprised looks on our American faces, she explains, "It is tradition in Germany to have *Kaffee und Kuchen* in the late afternoon. We will be pleased for you to join us."

It's a very sweet gesture of welcome and Mom says, "How kind of you! That would be wonderful."

The cake is warm and moist and gives me a much-needed energy jolt after the long drive from France. "This cake is yummy!"

Sebastian gives me a questioning look and says, "Yummy? Is that a good thing, Ellen?"

"Of course. It means that I like it very much!"

"And is our *Kaffee/Kuchen* tradition yummy too?"

I laugh and say, "What? No, only foods can be yummy."

I worry for a split second that I've made him feel foolish but he laughs too. "English, for me, has always new words to learn." He seems to think for a bit and then asks, "*Zoh*... do you *like* our tradition?"

"Yes. It's cozy and friendly."

Sebastian smiles and says, "In German, we say *Gemütlich*. You see? Now you have a new word too."

He's nice and seems kind of smart too. I think I'm going to like having him as my neighbor.

The whole family seems nice. With some pantomime and Sebastian and his grandma translating for his parents, I'm having a good time. However, my weird reaction at the entry is still bugging me so I ask his grandma, "*Frau Doktor* Müller, why does the sign by the door say *Haus Schumann*?"

"Call me *Oma* Sabine, Ellen. It's easier. *Na jah*... the sign says *Haus Schumann* because this house was built by my parents, Karsten and Anna Schumann. Papa is for a long time dead but my mama, Anna, has more than 90 years and she still lives here. She is now upstairs taking a sleep."

So... the house is named for her parents. There's nothing odd about that.

Oma Sabine then adds, "Your rental house next door is called *Haus Falke* because it was built by my grandparents, Christoph and Sigrid Falke."

I assume they're dead too since they'd be pretty ancient but I don't ask. Still, it gives me a bit of a chill that we'll be living in a house named for dead people… Yikes! What is wrong with me? I'm used to excavations once inhabited by dead people, right? That shiver by the house sign is creeping me out!

Turning back to the present, I notice that T.G. seems very quiet and kind of down. Dad's last assignment was in Italy and T.G. was so happy there that he didn't want to leave. When I see a tear run down his cheek, I wonder if that's the reason. Little Annika notices the tear too. She touches his arm and asks him something in German. To his utter mortification, he begins to cry and I hurt for him.

Without directly acknowledging T.G.'s meltdown, Mom and Dad make mutterings of the long drive and wanting to get settled and *Herr* Hofstetter hands over the key for the house next door.

As we walk over there, I take T.G. aside and ask, "Are you okay?"

"Leave me alone, Ellen."

Why are boys so uptight with their feelings? It's annoying and doesn't help to resolve the problem. I decide that it's up to me to pull him out of his funk. "You know, you weren't named after Alexander The Great for nothing! I've called you T.G. for a long time just because I think you *are* great!"

This makes him laugh… and ultimately talk. "It's just… I miss my friends Francesco and Andrea. And they weren't just my friends either; they were my soccer buddies. It was so cool when Italy defeated Germany in the Euro Cup and we were shouting *'Forza Italia!'* Now I feel like I'm in enemy territory."

"The Hofstetters seem nice though, don't you think?"

"I guess they're okay but that language… it sounds rough and hard to understand."

"Maybe Sebastian will help you. He seems good at languages."

"Hah! "

"What's wrong with Sebastian?"

"Nothing. He's just not like Francesco and Andrea, okay? Go away, Ellen."

I walk on thinking that I have three goals in my new country so far — to help T.G. through his homesickness for Italy, to find out if Sebastian is as interesting as he is nice and cute, and to figure out why I got that spine-tingling feeling outside *Haus* Schumann.

As Dad inserts the key into the front door of our rental, I notice a plaque similar to the one at *Haus* Schumann. It says, *Haus Falke, gebaut 1911.* I'm drawn to touch it and this time the shiver down my spine is more intense. Something is definitely *off* here.

Chapter 2 — Haus Falke

The entryway opens to a hall that smells like wood polish. On the left are a bathroom and a staircase to the second floor. Dad points straight ahead and explains, "That's the door to the kitchen."

So far, very exciting... Not.

Mom opens a door on the right and sounds happy, "What a lovely long living room!"

I peek in and then walk over to the large windows facing the backyard. There's no giant orchard like we had in Italy but we're in the city so I didn't expect one.

Mom is still gushing, "Oh, look at all the flowering bushes and plants! It even has a small pond!"

"The pond is supposed to have fish in it," Dad adds.

"Cool," yells T.G. "Let's check it out, Ellen." I follow him left into a dining room and out to the yard through some large glass doors. The pond does have fish and they're beautiful, shiny and big. Dad says they're koi. I have to admit this small city yard is better than I had hoped.

Inside, Mom leads us to the kitchen and starts going on again about how nice it is. I guess it's fine but I'm more interested in my own space.

After we climb the stairs, three big bedrooms and a large bath fill the second floor. Mom and Dad claim their room and then Mom says, "You two kids may choose between the other two."

There's no argument because T.G. likes the larger room and I like the smaller one with a better view of the pond. The only detractions are the piled boxes of our stuff that were delivered prior to our arrival but no problem — we're happy to have them!

Dad leads us to another staircase and I notice him smile. Before T.G. and I race ahead, Dad says, "The third floor is one of the reasons that I chose this particular house and I think you'll like it."

Instead of an attic, it's a finished suite with two rooms. Dad tells us, "You can use one room as a TV room, place to entertain friends, whatever. The other room can be used as a guest bedroom if you want to have friends sleep over. The only restriction is that if Cat is home from university it will be her bedroom while she's here."

That seems fair and I realize that I miss Cat already. It seems weird that I won't see her until Christmas. I'd kind of gotten used to having my sister around, even if she is a bit of a princess. Now that I'm fourteen, I was hoping that some of her style would rub off on me. I mean, I'm not beautiful like Cat and I don't want to obsess about clothes and watch my figure like she does but if I have any positive assets, I'll have no clue what to do with them. Cat would've kept me from looking like a total disaster… Whoa! What is wrong with me? It's not like I've ever worried about how I look! How pathetic am I becoming?

The last stop on our tour is the basement. Bor-ing! It's mostly storage space and a workshop. Mom's interest peaks however, when Dad opens a heavy door that reveals a sauna. "Oh Andrew, it will be such a welcome enjoyment during Munich's cold, damp winter."

As I move toward the stairs to leave the basement, I tell Mom and Dad, "I don't know about you but I'm not ready for cold and damp after sunny Italy!"

Halfway across the room, I feel a sudden chill. I get a weird feeling that something has happened in this part of the house. I shiver and try to ignore it but it's hard. First, the two signs gave off weird vibrations and now a spot in the basement is oddly cold! I try not to jump to conclusions but, given my history, it's just possible that I'm being given a mystery to solve. Two years ago in Cuma, Italy, an old prophecy that was made in Turkey before my birth took on a whole new meaning. This girl (me, Ellen Madigan) who loves science and is very practical, was predicted to be a psychic! Go figure. Anyway, I've always known some things that science couldn't explain but I pretty much kept them to myself up until Cuma — no need to cause people to think I'm weird, you know? In Cuma, I learned that I have a knack for getting in touch with the past and solving old mysteries. My family and friends witnessed it too and were amazingly supportive.

My Cuma experience was a bit daunting so I have mixed emotions about a possible new one. On the one hand, I love figuring out clues but on the other hand, I worry about the danger. Cuma involved some life-threatening situations. Still, maybe I'm overreacting. Aside from these spine-tingling shivers and chills, I haven't had any weird dreams or other psychic feelings since we left Italy.

I give myself a pep talk and some advice, "Calm yourself, Ellen. If it happens, it could be a wild ride but you can handle it, right? In the meanwhile, just wait and see what develops… but be prepared!"

Summer 1942 — Nazi Germany — A White Leaflet

It was lying in her path as she exited the lecture hall of the university and she would have stepped over it if the heading hadn't caught her eye. She bent over and picked up the leaflet, slipped it into her notebook, and headed for the tram.

Tired after the dry and complex chemistry lecture, she was grateful to find a seat for the twenty-minute ride home. She settled by the window and let her eyes close for a few moments. Her medical studies were rigorous and she welcomed the temporary break from work. Relaxation began to take hold but, at the next station, the tram jolted to a stop and her eyes flew open. More people got on and a middle-aged man slid into the seat next to her. His nearness and the loudness of his conversation with another man, resigned her to the fact that her peaceful alone time was over. She stared out the window and was mindlessly fidgeting with her notebook when she remembered the leaflet. Sliding it from the book, she began to read and then, realizing the dangerous line she was treading, quickly reinserted it. She prayed that her seatmate hadn't read the traitorous first line along with her — "Nothing is so unworthy of a civilized nation as allowing itself to be governed without opposition by an irresponsible clique that has yielded to base instinct."

She was still trembling as she entered her house and didn't take out the leaflet again until she was in the privacy of her bedroom, away from prying eyes. It was a brave and compelling piece of writing, given the times. It accused Germans of being spineless and urged passive resistance to "forestall the spread of this atheistic war machine." It urged those who sought freedom to make copies of the leaflet and distribute them.

By the time she was finished reading, her heart was pounding with a combination of pride and fear. She burned with admiration for those courageous enough to speak up this way, but she also sensed that they would be punished. She wanted to have the guts to make copies and add her voice to the opposition because Hitler's regime was evil, but she didn't know if she had it in her to be a martyr. After a night of anguish, she took a match to the leaflet and flushed the ashes down the toilet.

Chapter 3 — Marco

I wake up in a sweat shaking from the intensity. It's my first night in Germany and I'm having Nazi dreams! It's becoming clearer that it probably isn't my imagination running wild but it freaks me out all the same! Just like my Italian dreams, this one was very vivid and about someone's past life. The Cuma ones had been clues to an old mystery so I know that I have to take this seriously and keep my psychic antennae alert. However, I'm not going to say anything to anyone yet. Mom and Dad might worry and I don't even want to think about what my new neighbor, Sebastian, will think! I just get out my diary and start scribbling down every detail I can remember. When I'm done, I try to relax. I head downstairs for breakfast hoping for a relatively normal first German day.

****

Munich International School (M.I.S.) is south of Munich (or *München* as it's called in German) in a small farm community called Percha. Classes don't begin for two more weeks but Dad wants T.G. and me to see the campus where he has enrolled us and we need to go to a particular sports shop to pick up the required PE uniforms.

I've been looking forward to this visit but T.G. is miserable. "You've got to be kidding me! We have to ride over an hour on the school bus each way?"

Mom points out the panorama of the Alps as we head south on the Autobahn and says, "T.G., think how lucky you'll be to have that sight greet you every morning!"

He just burrows deeper into the seat and stares out the side window at the blur of Mercedes, BMW and Audi powerhouses that keep passing us.

When we get to the M.I.S. campus, Dad parks in the lot just inside the wall. From there, we walk up a tree-lined drive. The first building on the left looks like a fancy yellow cake decorated with white curlicues of frosting. Dad says that the turrets look Byzantine. I think it looks like it dropped out of a fairytale.

Dad explains that this small castle, Schloss Buchhof, is the Middle School and as a seventh grader, T.G. will have his classes there. However, T.G. is barely listening. He's much more interested in the soccer field opposite the Schloss.

We continue up the walk past the modern circular lower school. The buildings at the top of the rise are the gymnasium on the left and the upper school on the right where I'll have my freshman classes. The upper school consists of two long and narrow two-story rectangles that connect in the center. Dad says they look like Bavarian farm buildings. We enter the front door and head for the headmaster's office.

The meeting is brief and welcoming but also somewhat daunting. The headmaster wishes us well in our adjustment to both Germany and the school. However, he stresses that, although classes are taught in English, students from all countries are also required to study German. I notice T.G. cringe. The thought of learning to speak what he calls "confusing grunts" is not his idea of fun. I think learning German will be an interesting challenge though — especially if I can get Sebastian to help me.

When the meeting is over, we head into the nearby town of Starnberg where the sporting goods shop is located. While Mom and Dad pay for the navy blue training suits, white T-shirts and blue shorts, T.G. and I wander over to look at soccer cleats.

A boy with thick, straight, sandy colored hair is trying on a pair and, intent on lacing them, speaks in English to T.G. without looking up. "Do you play?"

T.G. is caught by surprise but he manages to mutter that he played right wing on his last team.

"I'm Marco... we could use a good attacker on the Middle School team. Are you any good?"

His directness might have thrown T.G. off balance except that the wide grin Marco aims at him makes it friendly. Extending his hand, T.G. says, "I'm Alex... I enjoy a good challenge." I sense the hope in his voice as he asks, "Marco... that's Italian isn't it?"

Marco laughs and says, "A lot of kids assume that, but no, my family name is Van Hoorn. I'm Dutch. Anyway, Marco isn't an unusual name in the Netherlands — one of the greatest Dutch footballers of all time was Marco Van Basten."

T.G.'s face lights up with recognition. He understands that Marco means *soccer* when he says *football* and he's well acquainted with Dutch Ajax soccer team players. He tells Marco that Ruud Krol, another Dutch great, once played for Napoli and had been treated like a hero there. Marco has some stories of his own and the two seem on their way to forming a friendship. T.G. seems reluctant to say goodbye when Mom comes to tell us that it's time to leave.

As we walk away, I say, "Since when are you called 'Alex'?"

He ignores me but I say, "Well, you're still 'The Great' to me."

As we eat our lunch by the town's lake, T.G. looks out over the water called the Starnberger See. Though tragedy comes to mind because it's the lake where mad King Ludwig is said to have drowned, T.G.'s personal dark mood has lifted. He tells me that this new place has possibilities. My dream flashes through my mind and I wonder what possibilities will be revealed to me.

Chapter 4 — Basti

I'm sitting on a rock in my new favorite place in the backyard and I've discovered that our pond has an interesting gene pool of fish. They are all the same kind (koi) but their skin varies in color and design. They're a bit like our family; skin, hair and eye colors are all over the place. Dad has pale Nordic skin, reddish hair and blue eyes. Mom has Latino caramel skin, deep black-brown wavy hair and brown eyes. Cat has fine straight blonde hair (like Dad's mom when she was young), Mom's brown eyes, and skin that is the golden-brown color some call *olive*. T.G. has Mom's wavy dark hair, Dad's blue eyes and skin that is neither cool Nordic nor warm golden — more neutral like the color of wheat. My own skin is *wheat* like T.G.'s and I have Mom's brown eyes. My thick, straight hair is a toned-down version of Dad's red — more like reddish-brown. We're not a boring group to look at and neither are the koi.

Absorbed with inventing names for the swimming creatures, a voice surprises me and I almost fall off the rock.

"Who is Harry?" I look up to see a scowling Sebastian hovering over me.

I point to a white fish with orange and gold marks. "That's Harry." Then realizing how foolish I must seem to be conversing with pond life, I feel myself beginning to blush.

"Did you name it after your boyfriend?"

I ignore that remark and say, "I've named all of the fish in honor of famous women archaeologists. Harriet Boyd Hawes was the first woman archaeologist to discover and excavate a Minoan settlement on the Greek island of Crete. Since I don't know if the fish is male or female, I call it 'Harry'."

Sebastian's face relaxes a bit and he kneels down beside me to get a better view into the pond. "Tell me the other names."

Sensing that he isn't going to mock me, I relax as well and point to a golden one. "That's 'Goldman.' It's named after Hetty Goldman who excavated in the Asian part of Turkey. That one that's almost completely white is 'Doughy' for Edith Hayward Hall Dohan, an expert in Etruscan objects. The all-orange one is 'Kenyon.' Kathleen Kenyon worked at Jericho in Israel."

"What about that one hiding under the plant?"

Surprised to have missed one, I move closer to Sebastian to get a better look. "I can't see another one. Are you sure?"

He leans in closer and tells me to follow the direction of his pointed finger with my eyes. They widen as I notice a small orange and white striped one and I find myself whispering. "Now I need to think of another name... I know. I'll call it 'Troy'! That's a site in Turkey not too far from where my Dad worked at Ephesus, just before I was born." Then as an afterthought, I add, "My middle name, Theodora, is Turkish."

Sebastian thinks for a moment and then whispers back. "The ruins at Troy were discovered by a German. These are German fish and yet none have German names. Why not call this fish 'Schliemann' after the archaeologist at Troy?"

I giggle and say, "Schliemann? That's a funny name for a fish!"

"What? And 'Doughy' isn't? I think that perhaps you don't like German names!"

I stop giggling and apologize saying, "I don't mean to hurt your feelings. I'm sure there are some great German names."

"Do you like the name Sebastian?"

"Sebastian is cool."

"*Fantastisch!* But you can call me Basti. All my friends do."

I feel myself beginning to blush again so I turn my face and get to my feet. As I walk toward the house, I hear him coming along behind me and I call over my shoulder, "You didn't tell me why you're here, Basti."

"I came to see your mother. My parents want to know if things are working all right."

I stop walking and turn to face him. This takes Basti by surprise and he barely avoids colliding with me. With my arms folded in front of me, I ask, "Why were you looking for my mother at the fishpond?"

A smile begins to spread across his face. "I saw your mother and she said everything was fine… except for you talking to fish in the pond. So, I came out. And see… it worked. Is it not better to talk to a real person?"

Despite the flush of pink that I can feel creeping up my cheeks again, I don't turn away. I have to laugh. Then I change the subject and say, "I wonder if German fish speak the same language as American… or Greek… or Russian fish. Don't you sometimes wish that people had a universal language and understanding?"

"*Du bist sehr tief.*"

"See? That's what I mean… no universal understanding! I have no idea what you just said. It's exasperating!"

"I don't understand this *exasperating* but if you had just asked me, I would have translated. I said, *you are very deep*, meaning…"

"I know what it means… and for your information, *exasperating* means *irritating*." Then, noticing the look of incomprehension on his face, I add, "You know… *upsetting*…"

"*Ah zoh…*"

"The fact that even you, with your good English skills, can't understand everything I say, emphasizes my point. As for me, I'm pathetic. I'm living in a country where I can't understand much more than food and hotel words!"

"You know what I think? I think that *Freundschaft*... *friendship*... is a universal language. We can use it to help one another understand German and English, no?"

I like where this is going and I answer, "Yes. But I warn you... I'm going to need much more help than you!"

"*Kein problem.*" Then, as if startled, Basti looks at his watch and explains that he is late for his tennis lesson at the Rothof. With a parting, *"Tschuss!"* he takes off.

I call to him, "I will call the fish 'Schliemann,' my new German word from you!"

Basti spins around and flashes me a big smile. "And I will call you 'Ellen Troy' so you remember your German connection!"

I laugh as I watch him wave and then hurry away to his lesson. I walk into the house thinking that a *Freundschaft* with Basti would be a nice way of navigating this new minefield of language and cultural challenges.

To my mom who is busy unpacking boxes I say, "Mom! How could you have humiliated me like that? Why did you tell him I was talking to fish?"

"But I didn't, Ellen. He asked where you were and I said outside, that's all."

I say nothing, but I feel a smile form. He asked where I was...

Chapter 5 — Two Hours

Our last days of summer vacation are filled with tram trips to the *Füssgänger* zone — a pedestrian area in the center of *München* filled with shops, cafes, and restaurants. Mom takes T.G. and me to *Kaut und Bullinger* for school supplies and to the large department store, *Kaufhof*, for new school clothes.

Mom means well but it's kind of embarrassing to be toted along like a little kid. T.G. and I envy the street action. Lots of kids our own age seem to be all around, meeting in small groups as they exit the subways, congregating around fountains, or shopping in trendy stores — all with no parents in sight. We see them at sidewalk cafes laughing, munching on street vendor goodies, and buying raffle tickets and redeeming them for little prizes. The city seems fun and safe. As we head home, T.G. and I agree that we can't wait to have some freedom to explore on our own.

****

School starts tomorrow and T.G and I are enjoying our last late morning breakfast for a while when Mom says, "I want to make one more shopping trip for underwear."

The mention of underwear, combined with having reached our shopping saturation point, has T.G. rolling his eyes back and me cringing.

"Buying underwear is sooo embarrassing, Mom! Can't you pick mine out for me?"

"I thought you might like to choose your own Ellen."

"Really? Let's see... spend my last day of summer vacation just chilling or shopping in crowds to find underwear? It's kind of a no-brainer for me."

"Me too," says T.G. "Besides, my old underwear is just fine. Most of my t-shirts only have minor holes."

Mom shakes her head, sighs, and warns us, "Well, just remember that, if you don't like what I pick out, you're stuck with it. I'm not about to make a second trip to return things."

Relief washes over me, and T.G. gives a one-fisted cheer. "Yes!"

My brother and I make solemn promises to stay in the neighborhood while Mom goes shopping without us.

Once she's gone, T.G. wastes no time. He gets his skateboard out of the hall closet and heads out the walkway. I run after him and try to call him back but he's too fast and I find myself abandoned. It's a bummer to be left alone but I resign myself to it and head back to the house.

Once again, I notice the sign by the door and, this time, I have a light bulb moment. It occurs to me that, though the date on this house says 1911, it doesn't look any older than Basti's house next door... and that one says 1952. Curious...

I walk back inside and, as I pass the cellar door, I'm overcome with a peculiar need to check out the basement again. As I head down the stairs, my sense of unease increases. I soon notice something curious on the walls; there is an obvious difference in color between the upper portions and the areas closer to the floor. I walk over and bend down to touch the mortar where the two sections meet. At first, I feel only the coolness of the stone but then I feel some inexplicable gentle force tugging at my fingers. I let them follow its pull and inch toward the back wall, sliding down and out to a spot on the floor that's obviously a section where the cement has been patched. My heart starts racing... is it fear? Or is it excitement at a new mystery?

What's just happened? My gut tells me that I'm supposed to do something here but what? Recalling the long-dead princess in Italy, I wonder if someone is buried in the cellar. It isn't my house so I'm not about to start making holes in it though.

I concentrate on calming down and thinking about a plan of action. Before I do any physical damage to the floor or needlessly alarm my family, I decide that I have to find out the house's history. For that, I will have to ask Basti — but without causing a fuss. I make a mental note of the location of the spot on the floor and head next door.

At *Haus* Schumann, I ring the bell. A tiny old woman with a braid of wispy white hair opens the door. The skin on her face appears almost see-through and has a web of fine lines. She has to be Anna, Basti's great-grandmother. She looks me over with milky blue eyes that seem to twinkle behind wire-rimmed glasses and asks, "Madigan?"

I nod and say, "Ellen." I ask, "*Frau* Schumann?"

She nods and with a frail whispery voice says something in German and motions for me to come inside.

I smile at her but hold my ground. Hoping she understands my English, I speak loudly and slowly, "SEBASTIAN... IS HE HERE?"

"Ah... Sebastian... Sebastian ist weg." Seeing my blank look, she shakes her finger and adds, *"Nein... nicht hier."*

I understand that *Nein* means *no* and my disappointment must show because she touches my cheek and then adds, *"Schau mal."* She points to her watch and makes a circular motion two times around, which I understand to mean two hours.

I nod, tell her *"Danke"* and turn away. As I walk back next door, I'm thinking that two hours is a long time when one has unanswered questions. I also think about the woman I just encountered. She's pretty ancient but dressed in clothes even my fashionista sister, Cat, would approve. Her slim black dress with white leather trim, the red silk scarf tied around her neck and even her walking cane with a colorful carved duck head are stylish.

At my house, I fill part of the wait time writing in my diary — not about a dream this time though. I scribble down my impressions of this new place I've landed. The last thing I write is a chart of the family next door. If my dream is connected to this house that their ancestors built, I figure it won't hurt to try and keep the generations straight.

Christoph and Sigrid Falke
great, great grandparents (built Haus Falke)

Anna Schumann
great grandma

Dr. Sabine Müller
grandma (Oma)

Silke Hofstetter (m. Franz)
parents

Sebastian (Basti) & Annika

Chapter 6 — A House's Story

I've been sitting by the pond for what seems like forever when I hear the doorbell ring. I sprint across the yard, through the house and thrust the door open to find Basti.

"Hallo! You were looking for me?"

I take in his tall athletic body, light brown wavy hair and fair skin with ruddy cheeks. He's still *fine* looking. That's all I can think about and it manages to make me tongue-tied.

I can feel the pink flush of my cheeks rising and it unnerves me. What is *wrong* with me? I shake my head as if to dispel an unwelcome substance, turn up my chin, and try to sound nonchalant. "Oh, it's nothing urgent. It's just that I was observing the basement..."

"*Ah zoh...* the deep one observes the basement."

He has an amused look that is sooo humiliating, but I plunge in anyway. "Was this house really built in 1911? I would have asked *Frau* Schumann but you know... the language thing."

Still smiling, he suggests that I show him what I've been observing in the basement. I'd feel a bit foolish except for the fact that my experience has taught me to heed signs.

In the basement, I point out the differences in the walls. No way am I ready to mention the force though.

"You are a very interesting person, Ellen Troy, and very clever... *sehr klug.*" He sits down on a bench outside the sauna, pats the seat next to him for me to come and join him, and then tells me a story.

"The original house was built in 1911 by *Uroma* Anna's parents, Christoph and Sigrid Falke."

"Aroma?"

"It's pronounced *UHR oma.* I don't know the English. She is the grandmother of my mother."

"Oh, your great grandmother — the one who opened the door for me."

"Yes, my great grandmother. By the way, she said to tell you that she apologizes for not speaking English to you. You took her by surprise and she does not speak it very often anymore."

"Anymore?"

"Like *Oma* Sabine, she is a medical *Doktor* and used it in her practice but she has been retired for a very long time."

"How old is she?"

"She has ninety-nine years."

"Amazing!"

"Yes, she is quite remarkable. Now do you want to keep asking questions or do you want to hear the story?"

"Sorry, just trying to get my facts straight. Please go on."

"During the second World War, this house was bombed. The only remains of the original house are the floor and the lower parts of the basement walls."

"Bombed! Was anyone killed?"

"Uroma Anna and her parents, the Falkes, were not at home. Her sister Elisabeth was not so lucky. She was here with her friend and both women were killed. The sad part is that the house had a bomb shelter but the women weren't in it."

My ears perk up at this bit of information. "Where was the bomb shelter?"

Basti stands up and walks over to the section of floor that is patched. "The bomb shelter was here. My *große Großeltern*... great great grandparents? had it filled in when the house was rebuilt after the war. I think they were bitter that it turned out to be useless."

"So if your great great grandparents went to the trouble of rebuilding this house, how come no one in your family lives here?"

"After my great great grandparents died, no one in the family needed it right away so they rented it out. Anna was their only living child and she and my great grandfather had *Haus* Schumann next door. By the time their daughter, my *Oma* Sabine, married my grandfather, Anna was a widow and they preferred moving into *Haus* Schumann with her. *Haus* Falke stayed rented. As a result, my mother grew up in *Haus* Schumann. When my mother married my father, *Uroma* Anna offered my parents *Haus* Falke but my mother says it didn't feel right; the family history is too sad for her. My parents chose to live in an apartment instead. After my grandfather died though, *Oma* Sabine and *Uroma* Anna needed help with house repairs and things so they asked my parents to move in with them. I've grown up in *Haus* Schumann too."

"What's it like having four adults always around telling you what to do?"

"Sometimes it's annoying but sometimes it's good."

"How?"

"Well, if I get in trouble with one of them, usually one of the others will listen and try to make peace."

"Make peace or get you out of being punished?"

"Hah! Let's just say I'm lucky."

I laugh but I'm thinking that he is lucky because they all love him. Then I change the subject. "Tell me about Elisabeth and her friend."

Basti doesn't tease me about having a morbid interest in the dead. He answers as if it's the most normal thing in the world. "If you are truly interested, I will tell you that story too, but not right now. I have to meet some friends in Schwabing and I'm going to be late."

I assure him that I'm very interested and then, not knowing what else to say, I mumble, "I guess you'd better go."

"*Tschüss,* deep one."

"*Tschüss.*" My attempt at saying good-bye in German makes him smile.

I wait until I'm alone and then, once more, go to the patch on the floor and touch it. This time I feel nothing.

As I climb the stairs, I realize that Basti didn't mention where the women are buried and I wonder if our house is a tomb. I shiver. Then I hear the door slam and T.G.'s voice calling me. His greeting is, "You'll never guess who I met!"

Summer 1942 — The Second Leaflet

She spotted the second leaflet on a bench in the university courtyard. Not daring to be seen picking it up, she sat down on top of it and continued an animated conversation with her friend Georg. They had just come from Professor Huber's philosophy class and a point that had been discussed troubled him. His voice picked up fervor and he practically shouted, "He lets his liberal viewpoint cloud his reasoning!"

She admired Professor Huber but something about Georg's rant sent a warning and she didn't feel comfortable revealing her true feelings. Trying the light approach, she teased him. "Na jah, Georg, it sounds like your romantic life!"

Georg laughed at this and praised her sharp wit. With a twinkle in his eye, he replied, "The study of Medizin requires anatomical research, no?"

As she laughed, she surreptitiously crumpled the leaflet. When he suggested that they get a Kaffee, she declined, mentioning a prior commitment. Kissing both of her cheeks, he whispered good-bye, "Tschuss!" As he walked away, she stuffed the wad of paper into her skirt pocket.

Back in her room that evening, she felt sick reading, "...since the conquest of Poland, three hundred thousand Jews have been murdered in this country." The author likened Nazi policies to a cancerous tumor that was infecting the body of the German people and scolded them for doing nothing. It said that it was "the holiest duty of every German to destroy these beasts." Once again, it urged the reader to make copies and distribute them. Although one particular message called out to her... "an end in terror is preferable to a terror without end," once again her courage deserted her and she burned the leaflet.

Chapter 7 — Routines

This time, I wake up from the dream wondering not only who the girl was but also who Georg and Professor Huber were. It's intriguing and I'm dying to share it but, for now, I only enter it in my diary. Before I head down to breakfast, I also update Basti's family tree with the new information about Anna and her sister.

Christoph and Sigrid Falke
great, great grandparents (built Haus Falke)

Dr. Anna (Falke) Schumann   *Elizabeth Falke*
great grandma (Uroma)   *(Liesi)-(died*

Dr. Sabine Müller
grandma (Oma)

Silke Hofstetter (m. Franz)
Parents

Sebastian (Basti) & Annika

This September morning is typical of my family's new routines. It's 6:30 am and Dad is having coffee before leaving for his new job at the museum and he's quite excited about the plans that are unfolding for the special exhibition. Mom is studying her German notes. She will leave the house at about 8:30 am for a class at the university. She always says that the best way to get the most out of a new cultural experience is to learn the language. She likes her class but admits learning German pronunciation and sentence structure is hard. Tell me about it!

It's a school day for T.G. and me too. We head out at 7 am to wait for the school bus with Marco Van Hoorn and his twin sister, Manon. (T.G.'s mood has improved ever since he met Marco skateboarding in nearby Arabellapark and learned that he lived close and would be taking the same bus.) The two boys introduced me to Manon the first day at the bus stop and I like her.

Today, Manon and I find seats on the bus together. Once the bus gets rolling, I tell her something I've noticed, "Manon, your English is amazing and, of course you speak Dutch, but I really envy how easily you speak German."

Manon smiles and twirls her finger around a strand of her thick sandy hair as she says, "It's just opportunity, Ellen. My father is Dutch and my mother is German so I have heard and spoken these languages since I was very young."

"Well my Mom is half Mexican and half Ecuadoran so I learned Spanish really young. That helped me learn Italian when we lived there but it's no use to me here."

"Well, at least we can speak English for now, Ellen."

"Thank God! By the way, how did your English get so good, Manon?

"Two words — international schools. My father manages hotels and we move a lot to many different countries. The one thing that most countries have is an international school and the common language is English. I've attended international schools since I was five."

"No way! So have I! I wonder if we've been to any of the same ones before this."

We spend the rest of the ride comparing schools and sharing the pros and cons of moving around so much. The ride seems to fly by and, as the bus comes to a halt in the parking lot of the campus, Manon says, "I'm sooo... looking forward to lunch today. *Germknödel* is on the menu."

"What on earth is *Germknödel*?"

"Oh, you have to try it, Ellen! It's a puffy dumpling with sweet vanilla sauce. Delicious!"

"Interesting. I'l check it out. Too bad we don't have lunch together. You could be my food guide."

Manon laughs and we get off the bus. I say goodbye to her and the boys. They head into the middle school and I head up the drive to my own building. T.G. has all of his classes with the twins except for his first year German. They also have a nice group of friends and he plans to try out for the soccer team with several of them. Since I'm two years older, I see Marco and Manon only outside of classes but that's okay. Freshman classes are a lot of work.

****

When the four of us get off the school bus in Arabellapark in the afternoon, we head into the Rewe supermarket and buy ice creams. This is my favorite time of day because Manon, Marco, T.G. and I get to hang out for a while. Sometimes we get a cheese-flavored roll called a *Käsestangel* at the bakery. Other times, we walk over to the Cadillac movie theater and make plans to see a weekend film. (It even has an old red Cadillac in the lobby.)

These after-school times are always fun but short. The long bus ride, after a full day of classes and after-school sports, means an arrival close to 5 pm. Lots of homework and dinner with our families mean that we have precious little free time during the week. This afternoon we lick our ice creams while telling stories about our day and sitting on a low cement wall. We make the ice creams last as long as we can before we have to head home.

****

On Saturday morning Mom and Dad go off to an outdoor market, the *Victualienmarkt*, for breakfast and shopping. As they often do, they plan to spend the afternoon either walking or bike riding in *München's* big park, the *Englischergarten*.

T.G., as usual, has gone to meet Marco and skateboard over the loop-di-loops among the walkways of Arabellapark. After that, they plan to go to the *Füssgänger* zone in the center to meet friends at the "Fish Fountain" in front of the old city hall at *Marienplatz*. Under the music and motion of the clock tower, they usually joke around and make spontaneous plans to check out music stores, grab a pizza, or to do whatever else pops into their heads.

Sometimes I hang out with them but today I plan to wander the city doing my own thing. I like to seek out bookstores that sell English-language editions so I can learn about the history of my new city or visit the places where historical events have taken place. Currently, I'm intrigued with places linked to the Nazis and I try to reconcile this clean and pleasant city with its sordid past. I've been to the *Feldherrnhalle* where a very young Hitler tried to overturn the government and to *Stadelheim,* the prison where those who were against the Nazis were executed during those dark days.

Today I'm heading to the university area by train where Mom told me there's a memorial to some students who opposed the Nazis. When I exit the *U-Bahn*, I find myself in a semi-circular plaza in front of the main building of the Ludwig Maximilian University of Munich. The plaza is named in memory of Sophie Scholl and her brother, Hans Scholl, students at the university during WWII. They were among the founding members of the White Rose resistance movement and were executed for writing and distributing anti-Nazi leaflets. I find stone copies of the leaflets, now embedded in the cobblestones, and trace them with my fingers while I contemplate the courage and risk of a precious few.

Across the wide boulevard is another semi-circular plaza and I wander over there. This one is named for a university professor who also resisted the Nazis as a member of the White Rose. His name was Professor Karl Huber... My heart races, as I make the connection. No way! The Professor Huber in my dreams was a real person!

It's a sunny beautiful day so I decide to walk for a while and think. The leaflets were written in German so I wasn't able to compare them to the two in my dreams. However, the fact that there were more than two leaflets on the plaza seems to be a sign that more dreams can be expected. It's exciting but also scary. Am I supposed to solve a Nazi mystery? Isn't that a bit much for an American fourteen-year-old? I suddenly feel like a whirlpool is forming around me ready to pull me into a new mystery, whether or not I'm ready — or even willing.

By the time I hop on a tram to take me home, my head is aching. I try to force my brain to switch subjects by people watching from my seat as the tram rolls past. It works for a while. I see an interesting mix of country people in traditional costumes, city people in green woolen coats, young rebels with multi-colored hair, tourists toting maps and guidebooks, students lugging backpacks, etc., etc., etc. I drink it all in and try to relax but I keep wondering how I'll fit in here, how I'll figure out where my dreams are pointing me and what I'll do about it.

Chapter 8 — Journal

It's on one of my Saturday tram rides that I run into Basti. He gets on with several of his friends and is so busy chatting with them that he doesn't see me at first. They're goofing around and I can hear the staccato rhythms of their German voices, punctuated with laughter. I grasp snippets of words familiar from class but not enough to understand what they're saying. Feeling every bit an outsider, I turn my head and gaze out the window. An overwhelming sense of loneliness overcomes me. I'm finding it hard to pierce the cliques in the upper school and I'm beginning to feel that I will never fit in.

I feel a hand touch my arm. "Hallo, Ellen Troy!"

As I turn, I feel a tear welling in the corner of my eye. Basti must see it because he asks if I'm okay. I nod and force myself to smile. Trying to sound confident, I answer, "*Spitze!*"

"*Ah, sprichst du Deutsch, jetzt?*"

"I'm learning, Basti."

Just then, one of his group calls to him. He yells something back and then the others get off the tram.

I'm surprised that he doesn't want to get off with them and I say so.

"Na jah, I see them all the time and I'll see them again at school on Monday. Where have you been hiding — not in the basement, I hope?"

I laugh and then explain about my long days. He's shocked because his own classes end at midday.

"Wow! That must be great, Basti."

"It's okay but I have *six* days of school, not five." He points to the load of books in his backpack and adds, "You see? I am now coming from my Saturday classes."

He slides himself into the seat next to me and we fall into easy conversation. I tell him about my morning and he tells me a funny story about his friends. Then, he changes the subject. "Ellen, my *Uroma*'s sister, Elizabeth, kept journals about her life during the war. Most of them are gone but my family has the last one she wrote. Would you like to see it?"

I feel my heartbeat quicken and say, "Oh yes, Basti! Of course I would!"

When the tram gets to our stop, we walk toward home together and agree to meet at the fishpond in the backyard.

****

The pages of the diary are yellowed with age but it has been stored in a Ziploc bag so that the loose pages don't fall out. The handwriting is well formed but written in pencil, perhaps due to the scarcity of ink during the war; Basti isn't sure. I scan the first page but the combination of the German language and the fading old style script make it seem like an unbreakable code to me. Basti sees the look of frustration in my eyes and says, "Not to worry, I will translate as best I can. Shall I tell you what I remember about Elisabeth from family stories first, Ellen?"

"Yes, that would be awesome, Basti."

"Her name was Elisabeth Beatrix Falke but most people called her Liesi and she was only 23 years old when she died in 1943. *Uroma* Anna was her older sister by five years. They were close though and both wanted to be *Doktors*. *Uroma* said she was fortunate to receive her medical degree in the early years of the war, but during Liesi's studies the war became so bad that classes at the university were shut down."

"So she didn't get to become a *Doktor* before she died, Basti?"

"No, but *Uroma* told me that, after classes stopped, another medical student, Magdalena Alt, asked Liesi to do some work with her for a *Doktor* Grüber. *Uroma* wasn't sure how Liesi and Magda spent their time but said that she was filled with her own fears in those days and didn't ask."

"Did her friend, Magdalena, become a *Doktor*?"

"No. It was Magdalena who was killed in the bombing with Liesi."

I absorb his words and then ask him where the bodies were found. His answer is a shocker. "No bodies were found except for two fingers that were identified as Liesi's. The blast must have been so big that the rest of the bodies were burned to ashes. They only knew of Magdalena's presence from the recovery of the identity cards of both women and the fact that, according to her mother, Magdalena had not returned home."

My inquiring mind finds it curious that two fingers and 2 identity cards could survive such a devastating blast when all else was pulverized but I hold my tongue. Something is definitely "off" but I need more pieces to begin putting together the puzzle. I'm anxious to learn what Liesi had written and urge Basti to read from the journal that Liesi started in the last months of her life. It begins with a poem.

"1 March 1943

Gray

Around my head the white flutters

Gray emotion

They are soon splattered red

Gray inaction

I am a healer who isn't healing. I am a student who isn't learning. I am a friend who can't be friendly. I am a woman who can't feel sexy or flirty or happy. I sense what's wrong, and it is like a cancer waiting to be excised. Yet I can't bring myself to operate.

8 March 1943

I look in the mirror and see nothing. There is no substance there, no spine, no heart, no soul.

13 March 1943

I am so lonely but these days, perhaps alone is better?

20 June 1943

The bombs keep coming and even in the shelter they sound terrifying. Perhaps they will erase my pain before I do it myself."

As Basti reads on, the entries are all similar. Liesi was very depressed, lonely, suicidal and seemed ashamed of something. There was also an unspoken yet pervasive feeling of fear.

The entries take on a different tone in August 1943, and Basti explains that it seems to coincide with her work with *Doktor* Grüber and Magdalena.

"10 August 1943

A little boy gave me motivation today and will perhaps save me from myself.

11 August 1943

I am exhausted but exhilarated because I have taken action.

14 August 1943

Children are the hope of Germany."

The entries continue in this more positive but somewhat vague manner. It was obvious that Liesi had found a purpose in her life, but she wasn't revealing it, even to her own journal. The unspoken fear was still hinted at. The last entry started and ended with another poem.

"1 October 1943

flight

Today

hunted caterpillars

food for scum

Tomorrow

fragile butterflies

But free from predators?"

I sit speechless for a few minutes and then ask, " Basti, when was the house bombed?"

"It was on 2 October 1943, Ellen."

His answer gives me a chill. "Basti, she wrote about flight and a new identity the day before she disappeared! It's so obvious to me that I can't believe it hasn't occurred to anyone else."

Basti looks at me in disbelief but then the importance of my words sinks in. In almost a whisper he asks, "Do you think she is still alive?"

"Perhaps we are meant to find out."

"*Du bist immer sehr tief,* Ellen Troy."

Chapter 9 — Sunday Morning Idea

On Sunday morning, Basti knocks on our door and Mom welcomes him with a smile. She likes Basti and, in her "mom" way, has said that he is "a well-mannered and personable young man." As he follows her into the kitchen, I'm just thinking that he is totally cute. Dad invites him to join us at the breakfast table and pours him a glass of orange juice. The mood is agreeable until T.G. asks him if he has come to check up on us. I can't figure out why T.G. is angry with Basti so I kick him under the table.

The coldness of T.G.'s voice must tell Basti that it isn't a friendly inquiry but he refuses to be baited and replies as if he hasn't caught the hostility. Pushing the truth a bit, he says, "Well, Ellen and I agreed to check up on each other's language and I'm hoping today is a good time."

I tell him that it sounds like a great idea but we're getting ready to head to *Walchensee*. "We've heard it's a beautiful lake surrounded by mountains."

"I know the lake well because I like to windsurf, Ellen. *Walchensee* is excellent for windsurfing because of the way the winds come off the peaks."

Dad laughs and says, "Windsurfing is beyond the experience of the Madigans so far. You might enjoy that T.G."

T.G. just glares.

Attempting to change the subject, Mom says, "Our plan is to take a chairlift ride to one of the peaks surrounding the lake. We'll hike the pastures, stop at a mountain *Hütte* for lunch and then hike down. The autumn weather is all blue sky and sunshine, so we're anticipating a great day."

If Basti is disappointed, he doesn't show it. He just asks to talk to me alone for a minute. I notice Mom and Dad exchanging amused glances but I don't care. I nod my head and say, "Why don't you wait outside for me and I'll meet you in a few minutes? There's something I have to do first."

I wait until he's out of earshot and then I lay into T.G.

Mom interrupts me saying, "That's enough, Ellen. Rather than making accusations about his rude behavior, we need to find out what's bothering him. We're ready to listen, Alexander."

He stares into his cereal bowl and says nothing at first. When he does speak, his emotions are raw. "Besides soccer, I feel that everyone in Germany is an expert in a lot of things I don't know how to do, like downhill skiing. It seems like all the kids at school are talking about it already. Some of my soccer friends were talking about the ski team and how they will travel to other countries to compete on the International School circuit. When winter comes, I'll probably have no friends! And now, here's another example — windsurfing! I feel like such a loser here!"

Dad reaches across and puts his hand on T.G.'s shoulder. "You are only a loser if you give up. You've never skied because you've been living in the south, but that doesn't mean you can't ski. With your athletic ability, learning should be a piece of cake! I'll bet you'll be flying down the slopes with a lot of your friends in no time. You don't think that we'd bring you to the foot of the Alps and not give you ski lessons, do you?"

T.G. looks up at Dad, shakes his head, and says, "I... I guess not."

"And one more thing. Don't be intimidated because people windsurf here. That's a water activity for these inland lakes. You've spent a lot of time near the sea and you've been surfing there. And did pretty well, if I remember right."

That last remark finally brings a smile to T.G.'s face and we're all relieved.

Outside on the front step, Basti apologizes for the secrecy but he says that he wants to share an idea with me and the thought of waiting till the following weekend is frustrating. I'm curious and I urge him to spit it out.

"I was thinking about *Doktor* Grüber and wondering if it might be worth trying to find him. I asked *Uroma* Anna if she had known him and she said she remembers him well. She doubts that he is still alive though because he would be over a hundred now."

"Bummer, but maybe he has family who can help us. Have you checked the phone listings?"

"No. *Uroma* says that he left the hospital during the war and she never saw him or heard about him again. She thinks that he either died or left Germany."

It sounds like a dead end but I can't give up. My curiosity is piqued so I tell him to wait there and I'll be right back. I'm about to head upstairs where the desktop computer is hooked up, but notice an old phone book on the hallway table. I grab it and return, saying "We may find nothing, but we've got to start somewhere… right?"

Basti grins as he takes the book I'm handing him and says, "*Uroma* says his first name was Heribert." His finger slides down the list of Grübers. There are quite a few but none listed under either Heribert Grüber or H. Grüber. The only *Doktor* listed is named Erika. Somewhat deflated, he hands the book back to me.

I think for a moment and then count the Grübers. "There are forty-two. At least one of them must be related to him. We could divide up the list if I spoke German but, unfortunately, you'll have to do all of the calling."

"Are you crazy? How will I explain forty-two phone calls on my cell phone bill to my parents?"

I screw up my face and begin wracking my brain for a better idea. "There's a public phone in Arabellapark, and I have ten Euros of my own money. That should let us make quite a few calls. If you meet me in front of Rewe tomorrow at 5, we can get started."

"5! I can't call people that early in the morning! They'll think I'm insane!"

"What are you talking about? I mean 5 pm... after I get home from school!"

Basti calms down and just shakes his head. "Fine. I'll meet you at *Siebzehn*... 17. In Germany we use twenty four numbers for the twenty four hours."

Feeling a bit dim-witted, I say, "I should know that from other places I've lived." Then I add, *"Bis Morgan,* Basti. Till tomorrow..."

This is followed by the sound of the front door opening. T.G. pokes his head out and mutters an apology for his rude behavior earlier. Basti makes light of it. *"Kein Problem!* I just thought you were a *Morgan Muffel...* a morning grump... like me before I am fully awake!"

After Basti heads home, Mom tells me to grab what I need for the hike and, before long, my family is off on our daytrip. As we head to *Walchensee*, I feel excited that Basti thinks my idea about Liesi's poem is worth pursuing. I just hope I'm right. A lot of questions swirl through my mind. Where is Heribert Grüber? Is he alive or dead? Will one of the forty-two names in the phonebook lead us to some answers about Liesi and Magda?

Summer 1942 — The Third Leaflet

She was having her lunch in the university Mensa when Georg and Uschi slid into seats beside her and thumped their trays down in front of them. Without so much as a greeting, Georg slapped a paper on the table and shouted, "Can you believe this treason? They are actually advocating sabotage of the party through 'passive resistance' and calling it a 'dictatorship of evil'! They even have the audacity to give suggestions!"

Uschi nodded in agreement and she added, "Our soldiers are dying for their country and anyone who doesn't support them should be shot as a traitor!"

It was the third leaflet that lay before her, and she was stunned. She burned to read the suggestions, for maybe they would motivate her to be courageous; but she dared not. She looked at her two normally rational and pleasant friends and wondered how they could live under the same horrifying conditions and not see the evil. She longed to say something to open their eyes but said only, "It's unbelievable, isn't it?"

Summer 1942 — The Fourth Leaflet

She was alone when she encountered the fourth leaflet, and she was successful in smuggling it to her room. This time it named Hitler and stated, "He means the power of evil, the fallen angel, Satan." It reminded the German people "... thousands fall every day in Russia..." but charged that German military successes were based on irrationality and evil. It urged German Christians to find strength in God to attack the evil that the Nazis personified. They were words that, if linked to an individual, could be fatal. This pamphlet, for the first time however, made it clear that it was speaking for a group. They identified themselves as "The White Rose" and emphasized that they were not in the pay of any foreign power. Though they assured their readers that their names were not recorded anywhere, and that recipients were random, she still destroyed the leaflet.

Chapter 10 — Phone calls

I head for the school bus with the latest dream tossing around in my brain. During the long ride, Manon catches up on homework and that's fine with me. I find a spot to sit alone for a while and I write the new details of the dream in my diary. What is it about this girl and the leaflets? Why does it matter now, so many decades later? Why am I, an American teenager, meant to be involved?

I also update the newest information on Basti's family tree — the fact that Liesi may not have died in the bombing!

Christoph and Sigrid Falke
great, great grandparents (built Haus Falke)

Dr. Anna (Falke) Schumann   *Elizabeth Falke*
great grandma (Uroma)   *(Liesi)-(survived?)*

Dr. Sabine Müller
grandma (Oma)

Silke Hofstetter (m. Franz)
Parents

Sebastian (Basti) & Annika

****

Monday seems endless to me. I can't concentrate in any of my classes, the after-school club isn't much fun, and even the bus ride home seems longer than usual, especially since neither T.G. nor any of our friends feel much like talking. To make matters worse, the drudgery will not end anytime soon; all of our teachers have piled on homework and it seems almost sadistic!

So, it's in a tired and foul state that I arrive in Arabellapark but, when I see Basti waiting for me, my mood lifts.

"Hey, Basti! Guess what? I got change at the school cafeteria so we have coins for the public phone and... well, I figured that a lot of public phones don't even have phonebooks anymore so I made a list of the forty-two names and numbers."

He takes the list and says, "I'm impressed with your efficiency, Ellen Troy. I didn't even think of a list. Thank you. I have some coins too but we can't use them in the phone. We have to use a phone card. Let's combine our money and get a card at Rewe."

****

The first name he calls is Adalbert Grüber but he can't help us. After six coins, we've had no luck. Not one of the people that he calls has any knowledge of Heribert, nor do any remember a physician in the family history.

The seventh coin results in a phone call that takes a long time. I'm pacing up and down on the pavement, hating not being able to understand the conversation and wondering what's taking so long with this one. After Basti hangs up, I ask, "So?"

"Are you free Saturday morning at ten? We have an appointment with *Doktor* Erica Grüber!"

I let out a yell and jump up in the air. Then I bombard Basti with questions and start with, "So, she's related to Heribert?"

"Yes. Heribert was her great uncle."

"Was?"

"He's dead now but we expected that right?"

"Yeah, I guess so but I was hoping he'd be the oldest man in Germany or something. Anyway, if we're going to meet her, she must know about his work, right?"

"Well she doesn't know much because he escaped from Germany and emigrated to the United States during the war and stayed there."

"If this is a dead end, why are we meeting her?"

I see a smile break out on Basti's face before he says, "*Doktor* Erika's papa is Heribert's much younger brother and he is still living. Though he is in his nineties, she says that his mind is clear and she thinks he may be able to tell us something about his brother's war work. If he agrees, she will bring him to meet with us."

"What if he doesn't agree?"

"She thinks it will be no problem so we will just have to hope it's true."

As we walk away, I feel a mixture of excitement and worry. I so want this to work out because, at the moment, I don't have any other options.

"All that telephoning has made me hungry, Ellen Troy."

I'm about to ask him how he can think of food when we're on the trail of discovery but I check myself when he offers to treat me to a snack. As we push open the door to Rewe supermarket, he asks me what I would like. I think of my favorite German candy and say, "I would love a *Kinderschokolade*."

Munching on our chocolate bars as we walk home, we brainstorm questions to ask *Doktor* Erika's father. When we get to *Haus* Falke, I thank Basti for all his help and say, "I have a feeling about this, you know…"

"I'm starting to believe in your feeling. *Tschüss*, Ellen Troy!"

"*Tschüss*, Basti!"

Chapter 11 — Heribert

A receptionist leads Basti and me into *Doktor* Erika Grüber's empty office and we wait. Sunlight from a tall window that overlooks a large square softens the dark wood-paneled walls. It's an impressive office in a smart section of the city. Looking around at the dozens of photos on the office walls, I sense that *Doktor* Grüber has a big group of family and friends. That's a good sign I think and I smile at Basti to reassure him. He seems nervous.

Behind us, we hear the door open and the woman who enters and shakes our hands isn't either young or old. *Doktor* Erika Grüber is pretty and fit with honey-colored hair and smooth skin. Under her open lab coat, she wears expensive looking clothes and jewelry. I wonder if I've guessed wrong about her because she hasn't brought her papa like she said she would. Not only that, her looks remind me of the devious Paola Chiaramonte who was involved in the crazy events at Cuma in Italy and I hope that *Doktor* Erika isn't untrustworthy too.

My doubts are erased when the door opens again and an elderly man joins us. *Doktor* Erika hugs him, helps him to a seat, and introduces him as, "My papa, Professor Karl Grüber."

It's obvious that the trip to the office has been tiring for Professor Grüber but his voice isn't frail as he asks, *"Zoh, was sind eure Namen?"*

Basti tells him his name and, when he introduces me, Professor Grüber immediately switches to English. I'm grateful and Basti says that it's fine with him. The professor isn't a grumpy old man either, because he smiles and says,

"You must be surprised to see an old guy like me with such a beautiful young daughter."

Of course we are polite and deny that we were thinking it, but it did cross my mind.

Despite our words, he feels compelled to explain. "I have the blasted Nazis to thank. Their murderous regime was afraid of thinking people and they cancelled classes just as I was about to start university. After the war, I got a late start to my studies and, by that time, I was motivated to educate others so it wouldn't happen again. I made no time for anything else until I had my doctorate and a teaching position at the university. I was 45 years old when I met my wife. She is younger and was able to present me with our beautiful daughter, Erika."

Doktor Erika kisses him on the cheek and then reminds him that it's time to answer our questions.

Basti and I take turns asking and Basti starts with the first one. "What kind of *Doktor* was your brother, Heribert, Professor?"

"Heribert was a pediatrician here in *München*."

I ask the next one. "Were pediatricians affected by the war?"

"Oh yes. When the Nazi policies of Hitler came into practice, Heribert became concerned with their effects on children. He saw the Hitler Youth groups as a way of educating a new generation of kids to hate. His particular

anger was with the children's transport program called
Kinderlandverschickung. The only good thing about it was
that it evacuated children from the war-torn cities to the
countryside away from the bombing. In reality, Heribert felt it
was also a means of educating children to become good
Nazis, away from the interference of parents and other
adults who disliked the Nazi regime."

"What did he do about it?" I asked.

"It was very dangerous to openly oppose things so he
just decided to make a difference for some of his own
patients. He faked their medical records to show illnesses
that would benefit from fresh air and rest and he was able to
prescribe suitable homes in the countryside. Suitable homes
for my brother meant homes free from Nazi ideology, but the
Nazis didn't know that — at least not at first."

I'm impressed so I ask, "Wow, that took a lot of
courage! How did he get them to the country and escape
Nazi detection?"

"There was a severe shortage of gasoline at that time.
Nevertheless, because of the necessity of caring for the war-
wounded, *Doktors* were allowed to have cars. Heribert took
advantage of this privilege to have his patients transported to
the countryside."

Basti is quick to ask, "Professor, we think that my
great grandmother's sister, Liesi, and her friend, Magda, may
have worked for your brother. Did you know them?"

"I didn't know them personally because I was quite young but I did know that he enlisted their help to take charge of the transport."

This last fact stuns Basti. He says that no one ever mentioned such a thing, and he wonders if the family knew about it.

I think of the words in Liesi's journal — "A little boy gave me motivation."

Professor Grüber continues. "The work was courageous. Traitors to the regime were being executed in those days and spies were everywhere. After only a few months, Heribert sensed that he was being watched and he began to worry for the safety of his operation and for the two young women doing the driving. He knew that they had to get out of the city and hoped to drive the three of them to safety in Switzerland. Their plans went awry when the Gestapo showed up at his house late one evening but luck saved him. He had just rounded the corner of his block when he saw the soldiers entering his building. He managed to get word to Magdalena and then sought a hiding place on foot."

The poem from Liesi's diary about flight flashes through my mind and I have to ask, "Did Liesi and Magda escape with your brother?"

"No, the two of them were supposed to meet him that evening at a wooded spot near the Isar River. My brother waited almost two hours past the rendezvous time, much of it cowering in the woods in fear, because a massive Allied carpet-bombing attack against the Nazis was underway. When the women didn't show up, he feared that they had been taken into custody or had been trapped, wounded or killed in the bombing. He headed south alone because he knew that he had to be gone before a daylight search for him began. He followed the river to an empty cabin many miles south of the city. It belonged to Rainer Koch, a friend of his. He reached the cabin and then, with the help of friends, made his way south and west — escaping in the dark, by boat, into neutral Switzerland."

"We thought he escaped to the United States."

"After some time, he did. Switzerland was neutral but German officers were free to come and go so they made it scary and stressful. Still fearing for his life, he made his way to Spain where he worked with the International Red Cross. Eventually, with his own money and the help of influential friends, he emigrated to the United States after the war."

When Professor Grüber finishes, Basti and I thank him and *Doktor* Erika and say good-bye. As we walk away from the office toward the tram, I realize that, though I had learned a bit about the Nazis in school, I had never met anyone who experienced their evil. To me, they were ancient history. I tell Basti, "I was surprised at how much the evil policies of the Nazis still seem to affect Professor Grüber."

Basti is quiet for a bit, and then his words are sobering. "Hitler haunts us Germans. If our family had Nazi members, we're ashamed. If they stayed silent despite knowing that Hitler was evil, we're ashamed. If we're unsure of how they acted, we're afraid of what we might learn. If they spoke out against the Nazis, they probably didn't survive and we're proud of their heroics but grief-stricken with our loss. I look around today and see so many good people but I wonder, *what about my friends, my teachers? What did their families do?* It's something that we don't like to talk about but it's always there you know — it is as you Americans say, the elephant in the room?"

I've touched a nerve, and I don't know how to respond so I decide to change the subject. "Basti, the one burning question that we went to find out hasn't been answered. What happened to Liesi and Magda? They may not have met up with *Doktor* Grüber but that doesn't mean they didn't escape from the house."

"Perhaps, but we may never know, Ellen Troy."

There seems to be very little to go on but the germ of an idea takes root in my brain. "Liesi and Magda might have known about the cabin, Basti. What if they got there after *Doktor* Grüber had left?"

Basti's eyes light up for a moment but then turn darker. "That still may not help us. The cabin was supposed to be empty. So, even if Rainer Koch is still alive, he may have no knowledge about whether they stayed there or not."

"But after arriving at the cabin, *Doktor* Grüber had help from friends. Perhaps *Herr* Koch, if he's still alive, would know who these friends were."

Basti smiles, takes me by the hand, and says, "They have computers in the public library and we can check all of Bavaria online for Rainer Koch."

The fact that Basti takes my idea seriously means a lot to me. I head to the library full of hope but with my fingers crossed because I don't want to let him down. It hard to focus though because *he's holding my hand!*

Chapter 12 — *Herr* Koch

We Google Rainer Koch in Germany and focus on towns south of *München*. We find a lot of Kochs but only one Rainer and he lives in the town of Wolfratshausen. I write down the address and phone number and then urge Basti to make the call.

"What will I say? Hallo! I was just wondering if you used to hide people from the Nazi Gestapo? He will slam the phone down for sure!"

That thought's a bummer for both of us. I sigh, put my elbows on the table, and sink my cheeks into my cupped hands. Basti narrows his eyes and thinks. Muttering that it requires a face-to-face meeting, he motions for me to wait and then goes online again. He finds a street map of Wolfratshausen and searches for the location of Rainer Koch's home. When he's done, Basti looks up and asks, "How do you feel about taking a ride on the number-seven *S-Bahn*, Ellen?"

"I don't know. Why?"

"It's the commuter train that travels to Wolfratshausen."

I grin, slap Basti a high five and we're out the door in a flash. It takes us about an hour to make the trip from *München* and it's early afternoon when we arrive. Wolfratshausen is busy with Saturday shoppers, many of them scurrying to finish their purchases before the early closing time. Some are carrying baskets filled with market veggies and others are toting shopping bags with the labels of local shops.

The Koch residence turns out to be an apartment located over a *Holzschnitzerei*, a shop that makes and sells woodcarvings. The top half of the building front has a large painted scene that's pretty cool. Basti tells me, "It's called *Lüftmalerei* and it's a traditional alpine art."

We ring the bell at the apartment entrance to the right of the storefront. No one answers so we decide to ask at the shop. The counters and shelves are crowded with beautifully crafted wooden pieces and a guy sitting in the rear is busy carving, absorbed in his work. He doesn't seem to hear us so Basti shouts out a typical Bavarian greeting, *"Grüss Gott!"*

The carver looks up with a startle and then smiles and returns the greeting. Putting aside his work, he gets up and comes forward, asking if he can help us find anything in particular. Basti explains that we're looking for Rainer Koch.

"Ich bin Rainer Koch."

Basti tells him that he's too young. The man's face breaks into a lop-sided grin and he says something that I don't understand. After Basti replies, he turns to me and translates because he can see that I'm bursting to know. "*Herr* Koch said that, at 52, it has been awhile since anyone thought that he's too young."

I smile with politeness but I'm anxious for answers. Basti senses this and turns back to *Herr* Koch. He explains that we're looking for someone older with the same name — someone perhaps in his 90's. I hear *Herr* Koch say the word *Großvater* which I know means *grandfather* and I get my hopes up. Basti's translation is a bummer though; his grandfather, also named Rainer, is dead.

"Basti, ask him if he might have any helpful information anyway."

Questions and answers go back and forth and I recognize shock on *Herr* Koch's face as he nods. I realize that I'm holding my breath as I wait for the translation. Basti tells me, "I asked him if his grandfather ever had a cabin near the river. *Herr* Koch said, 'yes' then asked how we knew and why we were interested, so I told him the story."

Herr Koch watches us as Basti explains and then interrupts again. Soon Basti is smiling but I don't know why. I hate not understanding the language! At last, Basti explains, "*Herr* Koch's papa might be able to answer our questions."

Yes!

My excitement fades as he adds, "There is one small problem, however. He can't do it now."

"Are you saying that we have to come all the way back here another time?"

Basti smiles and says, "No. *Herr* Koch says that he needs to tame the hunger in his belly first and we are welcome to join him upstairs where his wife will have the midday meal prepared. After that, we can listen to stories of the past."

I realize that I haven't eaten anything since early morning and that my own belly is beginning to rumble but I tell him to ask if it will be all right with *Herr* Koch's wife.

Basti says he has already asked and it's not a problem. *Herr* Koch assured him that she wouldn't mind two more mouths to feed.

"Great! Tell him 'Yes'!"

With a laugh, he says, "I'm very hungry so I already said yes."

After *Herr* Koch closes up the shop, he motions for us to follow him upstairs. As he opens the door to the apartment, we're met with tempting aromas but *Frau* Koch is nowhere to be seen. Her husband assumes that she has made a last minute run to one of the shops and will be back soon.

Just then, an older man comes into the room and *Herr* Koch introduces us to his papa, Helmut. Then he points out the washroom and suggests that we freshen up while he explains to his papa what we need.

As he predicted, his wife comes bustling in just a short time later and she sets out two more plates without batting an eye.

After steaming plates of pork cutlets and some cheesy noodles called *Käsespätzle* are eaten, Rainer's papa is ready to tell us his story. Out of respect for me, he offers to speak slowly and make pauses so that Basti can translate as he goes along. It's a generous thing to do and I thank him, *"Danke schön."*

Herr Helmut says that it's *Kein problem* and then he begins. "The cabin was on the riverbank a bit north of Wolfratshausen. My papa, Rainer, was also a wood carver and he worked out of the cabin and sold to merchants who traveled on the river."

After Basti translates, I say, "Ask if the business was affected by the war."

The old man's reply is interesting. "No. The war didn't matter to his business because he stayed out of politics most of his life and, at age 30, he hoped he was too old to be drafted. However, as Hitler and the Nazis became more and more powerful, he worried about the impact on me. As a nine-year old, I would soon be required to join the *Deutsches Jungfolk* to begin my Nazi indoctrination. He didn't want that to happen but fear led him to do nothing for a long time."

Basti translates again and I say, "Ask him what made his father decide to act."

"Ah zoh, it was because of *Doktor* Grüber. He was Papa's childhood friend and he offered a solution. He listed me as a patient with lung problems so I could be included in his medical relocation program. Then he took me by car to the home of *Herr* und *Frau* Schiller in Mittenwald who gave me home schooling in the fresh country air. Papa was grateful, not only that I would be away from the Nazi-run state schools but also because I would be further away from the bombing and at least a little safer."

When Basti explains, all I can think is, a little *safer*? I can't imagine my whole childhood being lived in fear of Hitler and his Nazis. A whole generation of kids had to be careful of what they said and did for fear of death. Even if they got lucky like *Herr* Helmut and were relocated by *Doktor* Grüber, the danger was still there. Then another thought occurs to me; *Herr* Helmut said his papa was afraid and yet *Doktor*

Grüber went to him for help. I urge Basti to ask what happened.

Helmut Koch considers the question for a moment and then says, "When *Doktor* Grüber thought that the Nazis were on to him, he made a frantic phone call to Papa asking to use the cabin for one night. He and his two assistants planned to flee to the south and needed a stopover. Papa was afraid but two things made him say yes. First, he wanted to repay the *Doktor* for saving me. Second, *Doktor* Grüber made it almost risk-free. He told my parents to make plans to be away and make sure that others knew it. That way, if they were caught, it could be assumed that they had trespassed into the empty cabin."

That made me blurt out, "But how could your parents be sure that the three of them arrived?"

Herr Helmut explained, "*Doktor* Grüber said he would do something to signal that he had been there. He asked my parents to lean a broom against the outside of the cabin to the left of the door. If all went well, it would be moved to the right side. Trouble would be indicated if it were knocked to the ground. When they returned, it was on the right."

Basti is excited. "So, they had evidence that *Doktor* Grüber and his two assistants had been there!"

"Well, no. They thought so but a couple of days later my parents had a surprise."

At this point, the old man stops speaking, as if for dramatic emphasis and to give the statement time to sink in. Basti and I can hardly contain our curiosity, and I feel myself tense in anticipation.

Herr Helmut seems to be lost in his own thoughts for a bit but then he continues the story. "Two young women appeared at the cabin door late one evening looking bone-tired, fearful and hungry."

I notice Basti tense as he asks, "Do you remember their names, *Herr* Helmut?"

"They told only their first names, Liesi and Magda."

Basti yells, "You were right, Ellen Troy! They didn't die in the bombing!"

I shout, "Yes!" and then notice that the Kochs are looking at us funny. *Herr* Helmut asks why we are happy when the women were in terrible shape.

Basti is quick to explain, "We are happy that they were alive, not that they were tired, fearful and hungry."

The old man nods and then says, "They were in worse condition than that. My mother saw that Liesi was badly wounded and seemed to be upright only with the support of her friend. Without asking questions, she whisked them inside, eased Liesi onto a bed, and then went to get Papa. He was alarmed that strangers had shown up and hurried to speak with them. After he determined that they were *Doktor* Grüber's assistants traveling alone and to their knowledge had not been followed, he relaxed a bit."

I can see that Basti looks worried as he asks, "How bad was Liesi?"

"She was feverish and had a filthy bloodstained rag on her left hand. Papa asked Magda what had happened and upon learning that parts of two fingers had been lost during a bombing attack, he realized that she required medical attention from a physician — but one who could be trusted. Magda's medical training had kept her friend alive up until then but she was too exhausted at that point to provide more care."

I ask, "Was your papa able to get her a *Doktor*?"

"Papa could think only of *Doktor* Söllbach in Mittenwald. It was quite far but he called anyway. *Doktor* Söllbach had a friend not too far from Wolfratshausen who was a nurse and he promised that she would be there soon. Realizing the danger that both the women and my parents were in, he also promised to see that the women were transported further south in the early morning."

I press on with another question, "Did the nurse come and did she help Liesi?"

"Yes. It was dangerous for her also because there were curfew rules at night. However, before long, a sturdy woman carrying a market basket with a loaf of bread sticking out from the top, knocked at the door. Hidden beneath some other food items, she had first-aid supplies for cleaning and dressing the wounds, as well as an assortment of medications. She got to work and soon had Liesi more comfortable and in less danger of infection. She said it would do until a *Doktor* could treat her."

At this point, the old man says that he needs to get some water. Basti offers to get it for him but he says that a little walk to the kitchen will ease his stiffness. Basti and I wait but we're not patient because we're anxious to learn more about Liesi and Magda's ordeal.

After a short break, *Herr* Helmut returns and resumes his story. "After the pain medication took effect and Liesi was asleep, Magda filled my parents in on what had happened to Liesi and herself. After the warning from *Doktor* Grüber, Magda arranged to meet Liesi at her house. From there, they planned to set out together to meet the *Doktor* and make their way to the cabin. As the two women were preparing to leave however, Allied bombers attacked *München* and Liesi's house was leveled. Liesi and Magda managed to make it to a shelter in the basement but only after Liesi's left hand was maimed in the bombing, severing parts of two of her fingers. Magda wanted to try sewing the fingers back on as she had observed during her medical school training but Liesi had a more daunting idea. She would leave the pieces of her fingers for rescue workers to find, hoping that they would assume she was dead and thus give the Gestapo no reason to look for her. Since no one had known that Magda was in the house, they decided to leave her identity card, hoping that she too would be presumed dead. Then, fearing that the fingers would be presumed to be Magda's, Liesi left her own identity card as well and the two women clawed their way out of the rubble and hurried off into the night."

At this point, I'm feeling a bit nauseous. Liesi must have been desperately afraid to choose to leave her two fingers. It must have been bloody and unbearably painful! I look at Basti and see that he is deeply affected too. *Herr* Koch notices our distress and offers to stop. No way are we not going to hear him out though, so we urge him to continue.

"It took Liesi and Magda three days to reach the cabin, traveling only under the cover of darkness. During the day they hid in the woods and in barns. They drank river water and ate berries but that wasn't nearly enough. Liesi was weak and feverish and Magda worried that Liesi's wounds would fester. *Doktor* Grüber had explained the location of the cabin in case they became separated so she made that their goal. Magda hoped to figure out a way to get help once they were there. The realization that the cabin was occupied frightened her, but with Liesi's condition deteriorating, she decided to take her chances. She thanked God that my parents came to their rescue."

Herr Helmut grabs his water glass while Basti and I also sip some water and take the time to talk a little. We agree that Liesi's condition sounded bad and Basti whispers, "I wonder if she survived the night and traveled further."

"I hope so, Basti, but I wonder how much blood you lose when part of your fingers are cut off!"

We are both feeling pretty sad when *Herr* Helmut continues. "Just before sunrise, a hay wagon stopped in front of the cabin and the driver came to the door. It was *Doktor* Söllbach dressed as a farmer! He had driven much of the night and said that he was anxious to get going again without delay. He evaluated Liesi's fitness to travel and deemed her fragile but he felt that her life was in more danger if she stayed put. He and Papa made a hole in the hay pile that was in the back of the truck. Then they bundled Magda into a sack and placed her into the opening. Away from prying eyes, she was able to free her head and arms while waiting for them to return with her friend. When Liesi was eased in beside her, she freed her friend's head as well, and the men covered the both of them with hay. 'Farmer' Söllbach then mounted the driver's seat and headed south. The plan was for the women to be hidden in the *Doktor's* barn until Liesi was strong enough to travel further."

When *Herr* Helmut is finished, Basti's stunned voice whispers, *"Mein Gott,* Ellen Troy, could they still be alive?"

I whisper back, "If they are, why haven't they come home?"

Turning once again to *Herr* Helmut, Basti asks him if he knows what happened to the women after that.

"Papa never said. Perhaps he didn't want to know. It was safer that way, *gelt?*"

I prod Basti to ask if *Doktor* Söllbach is still alive. He isn't. *Herr* Helmut was told of his death while he was still a boy living with the Schillers in Mittenwald. Oskar Söllbach was executed for treason in early 1945, after someone told the village Nazi watchman that he refused to return the *Heil Hitler!* salute. After that, the advance of the Allies was the only thing that eased the fear of young Helmut and his temporary guardians, *Herr* und *Frau* Schiller.

Basti and I try not to show our disappointment as we thank the Koch's for their hospitality but the taunt of being so close to a trail and then having it dead end is frustrating. As we turn to go, *Herr* Helmut offers one last morsel; *Herr* und *Frau* Schiller are still alive.

So our quest is still alive too!

****

It's almost *sechzehn,* (16, or as I like to say, 4 pm) when the *S-Bahn* pulls into *München* and our two tired bodies push forward to find a tram. I know that my parents will be wondering why I've been gone all day.

"Basti, we have to get our stories straight because this morning, I only told my parents that we were going downtown."

"Yah, but we haven't done anything wrong, Ellen Troy."

"I know, but I don't want to risk messing our investigation up by telling them what we did and getting grounded."

"Okay. Let's just say that our day was spent exploring the city and having lunch with friends. It's true; it just leaves out some things."

"Perfect. Now, what's our next move, Basti?"

"Mittenwald, where the Schillers live, is beyond the reach of the *S-Bahn* system so we can't make a quick daytrip down there by ourselves. We will have to convince one set of parents to drive us there."

"How can we do that without telling them why, Basti?"

"I'm not sure. It's a picture postcard tourist town but they know that teenagers hate sightseeing. It will make them suspicious. It's also known for violin making but neither of us is particularly musical. I'll have to think about it."

Basti squeezes my hand and whispers that he's sure we will find a way to proceed further. At this moment, I almost don't care where we will proceed as long as it's together. My sensible side wants to slap myself for focusing on unimportant things. My heart whispers that certain people can be important too.

January 1943 — The Fifth Leaflet

She had seen no more of the defiant but inspirational writings for months – since the end of July, in fact. All through the autumn and into the winter there was nothing, until now. "A Call to All Germans!" was how the fifth leaflet began. It stressed that the end of the war was nearing and it was not too late to prevent Hitler from leading them all into the abyss with him. It implored people to "Dissociate yourselves from National Socialist gangsterism. Prove by your deeds that you think otherwise." Once again, it urged, "Support the resistance. Distribute the leaflets!"

Something in those words moved her to tears and this time she resolved to find a way to lend her support. She knew that she couldn't be the only medical student who felt this way and she reasoned that some of her classmates must share her disgust for Adolph Hitler. After all, medicine, by its very nature, should attract compassionate and humane individuals. Finding that kindred spirit became her self-appointed task.

During a biology lecture the next morning, she found it hard to concentrate on the science. She studied the faces of her classmates and considered their political leanings. Whoever she approached would represent a calculated risk but she hoped to narrow the odds through careful selection. Some had, like Georg and Uschi, openly declared their support for Hitler and others had merely hinted at their acceptance of the regime. Some of the male students had been quiet about their views but had served with the German medical corps on the Eastern front when they were drafted. She wasn't sure if that signified compliance with the regime or just responsiveness to their medical calling. In the end, she would have to go with her gut. Eliminating those whom she considered too timid or too abrasive and those who had relatives connected to the regime, she picked three individuals to hone in on. She would first feel out Katja Bauer who seemed easy to talk to. If that didn't work out, she planned to approach Magdalena Alt and her last resort would be Christoph Probst. Of the three, he seemed the most compassionate and perceptive but he had a pregnant wife and two children and she doubted he would want to take chances for their sake.

She approached Katja on the way out of the lecture hall and bemoaned her own difficulty understanding one of the lecture points. Katja commiserated and suggested that they go up the boulevard to one of the cafes and compare notes. After wading through the intricacies of cell structure, they relaxed and enjoyed some "girl talk," evaluating the eligible men they both knew. Then something triggered an alarming note. Katja claimed to be attracted to Alex Schmorell but she began by questioning his German allegiance. "Don't you think it's odd that a boy who is half Russian would serve as a German medic on the Russian front? He doesn't seem as committed to medicine as the rest of us either, what with all of his interest in music and art."

Was Katja fishing for some sort of incriminating evidence? Was she a party spy? It made the fear in her electric but she struggled to remain cool and said, "Hör mal, Katja, Alex was a brave German medic and saved the lives of countless German soldiers. He didn't shrink from his responsibility and he shouldn't be faulted for his dead mother's heritage. He will be an excellent German physician like his papa." With a forced smile on her face, she added, "Let's face it, Katja, it's the romantic Russian artist in him that you find so attractive, isn't it?"

Katja forced her own smile and replied, "Na ja, you're right."

The subject was changed and they soon said good-bye.

After that strange encounter, she began to doubt her judgment of people. She had lost the courage to approach Magdalena but they had a chance meeting in a bookstore. It was Magdalena who initiated the conversation and suggested that they have Kaffee und Kuchen. She knew a place that had real Kaffee, a welcome relief from the brown water brewed from acorns that wartime rationing had necessitated. Even the Kuchen was made with real butter, she assured her.

Their conversation jumped from one non-controversial topic to another but she felt her nerves on edge just the same. After they poured themselves a second cup from the little pitchers on the table, Magdalena abruptly asked, "What do you think of the leaflets?" and she almost spilt her Kaffee. Not waiting for an answer, Magdalena continued. "I think it's terribly brave, don't you?"

She was frozen with indecision. Was this a fishing game that would result in a trap or did Magdalena believe what she was saying? Casting her lot, she whispered, "Yes, it's very brave." Within seconds of saying it, a male voice broke the silence. It was Georg. "Grüsse, Lieblings! How's it going? What are you up to?"

His voice, and the remembrance of his condemnation of the leaflet, closed something off in her. She said, "Nothing much. In fact, I was just going." She turned to a somewhat ashen Magdalena, told her how much she had enjoyed the conversation, left coins and ration coupons for her half of the bill, and headed out the door.

Chapter 13 — Interlude

The demands of school and family things fill the days for me but I can't get the newest dream revelation out of my mind. The appearance of Magdalena Alt has been a shock and I'm starting to believe that the dreams are truly about Basti's grandaunt, Liesi. It kind of makes sense because the dreams started about the same time as the strange vibes I got when I was in the basement of her house. I want to tell Basti but I'm afraid he will think I'm a total weirdo. Besides, Liesi's name hasn't been mentioned in the dreams. So, I decide to continue keeping the idea between me and my diary, at least for the time being.

I manage to see Basti on weekends. He introduces me to the Cosima *Wellenbad*, a public indoor swimming pool with mechanical waves that is just down the road.

I tell him, "It's so cool that you can swim through a little tunnel that goes from indoors to outdoors!"

" Even on cold days it's no problem, Ellen Troy, because it's heated. People enjoy it all winter long!"

Basti also introduces me to Spaghetti Eis, a vanilla ice cream concoction that is squirted out onto a dish to make it resemble a plate of spaghetti! The red fruit topping even looks like tomato sauce.

He tries to get me interested in his favorite old-school German singer, Udo Lindenberg but he's not my thing.

I tell him, "I prefer more current stuff but I kind of like some cheesy old music. It makes me laugh."

One day in early October Basti says, "It's Oktoberfest time, Ellen Troy. Let's go to *Theresienwiese* and see the gigantic beer tents."

"We're too young to drink beer, Basti!"

"Yes, but it's fun to sit on the hillside and watch the mobs of crazy celebrators from all over the world. They usually eat and drink too much and then try to sing and sway to the music of the brass bands."

We do go, and watching from the hillside is fun but I also enjoy the carnival rides and peeking into tents with beer names like Augustiner, Hacker, Löwenbräu and Schottenhamel. The dirndl-wearing waitresses are amazing as they heft multiple liters of the foamy liquid in each hand!

At quieter times, I ask Basti if he has come up with any ideas for getting to Mittenwald but he always answers, "Not yet" — the unspoken part being, *but I will*. I have no doubt that an idea will surface in time so I don't push him.

Munich International School has its fall break in late October and Mom, T.G. and I have an opportunity to accompany Dad to Greece. He has appointments in Athens at the National Archaeological Museum and we are free to enjoy the city. I usually like such trips but this time I think of it as lost time from the mystery Basti and I need to solve. Basti needs to do it for his family and I need to follow the signs that are my gift and to satisfy my curiosity.

Wandering around the pedestrian alleys of the *Plaka* district in Athens which is filled with tourist shops, cafes, restaurants, musicians and street vendors, I buy two pair of worry beads — one for myself and the other for Basti. Perhaps they will help us to concentrate on finding an answer.

As October turns into November, the air turns crisper and the scent of roasting chestnuts fills the *Füssgänger* zone downtown. Then on December first, things really get festive with the arrival of the *Christkindl Markt,* the annual month-long outdoor Christmas fair. I've been looking forward to it and I make sure to be there on the first weekend. It's so much fun that I look forward to going again.

When Basti suggests that we go together on the third Saturday of December, I'm happy. The city seems alive with the Christmas spirit as we wander between the wooden stalls. The aroma of *Glühwein* and sugared nuts is sweet and strong but we feed our hunger with Currywurst and french fries. As we surf our way through the crowds looking at the stocking stuffer trinkets and carved wooden Nativity figures, a light sprinkling of snowflakes descends upon the city. We're giddy with the charm of it and begin to twirl about and try to catch the flakes on our tongues. In the midst of our playing, Basti shouts, "That's it!"

I stop twirling and stare. "What's it?"

"Snow! It's our answer!"

Thinking that perhaps he has sneaked some of the alcoholic *Glühwein* when I wasn't looking, I lean against a building and motion for him to join me. I ask, "Are you okay?"

Basti can't stop smiling and says, "You think I'm crazy, but I'm serious. Mittenwald has skiing. What better reason to visit? No?"

I feel as if my heart is about to collapse. "But I don't know how…"

"It may be the perfect reason to get my family to invite you along. Everyone who comes to Bavaria should at least give skiing a go! I could offer to help you get started. What do you think?"

My heart fills up again. Using a new German word for *awesome* that I have just learned, I smile and shout, *"Toll!"*

Chapter 14 — Mittenwald

The snow flurries in mid-December are fleeting. *München* is forced to endure a damp and gray holiday season weather-wise.

"Ugh! I hate this weather!"

"Now, Ellen, try focusing on how much you have to be joyful for. We have a warm house, good friends and each other."

"I know, Mom. It's just depressing, you know?"

Dad overhears us and says, "I have just the cure for a depressing Sunday. How about we all go out and pick up a real Christmas tree? This weather is perfect for keeping them fresh."

I laugh and say, "Remember how all the needles fell off our tree in Italy after only a week? I love warm weather but not for Christmas."

By the time we get back, my blue mood has lifted and I even offer to help Dad untangle the lights we had stored in the basement. Mom serves us all hot cocoa and she and T.G. and I watch Dad string the lights on the tree. When they are lit, I whisper, "It looks magical."

As Dad and T.G. drag over the box with the ornaments we've saved, Mom gets up from her chair and says, "I have a surprise. I've bought some German ornaments for us to add to our old ones. Ellen, will you help me fetch them from upstairs?"

When we return, I help Mom open the new ones. There are tiny wooden figures, cookies in the shape of trees, wreaths and stars she calls *Christbaumgebäck,* straw ornaments, and real candles that are attached with clips on metal candleholders. Always safety-conscious, Dad insists, "The candles have to be left unlit. There's no sense risking a fire," and none of us object because they are pretty cool, even without flames.

After the tree is trimmed, Mom asks T.G. and me, "Would you kids like to help make *Lebkuchen* cookies?"

T.G. seems unsure as he asks, "What are they?"

"You'll like them," I assure him, "They're gingerbread and you like anything that's edible."

He laughs, we all get to work and none of us worry about the weather.

****

Cat, is home from university. She came from Paris by train a few days ago and she made quite an entrance onto the train platform, dressed all in black looking fabulous as usual and squealing hellos in French. Mom and Dad were suddenly *maman* and *papa*.

When she called T.G. *mon petit frère*, he answered, "Say what?"

Mom leaned over and told him that Cat called him "little brother."

T.G. grinned and said, *"Ah, meine große Schwester!"*

That got Cat all in a French snit and she said, "I am not gross! And I'm not schwes... whatever!" Her new Parisian sophistication crumbled as she yelled, "You, T.G., are *un enfant terrible!*"

T.G. yelled back, "I'm not an infant!"

Mom stopped the family reunion from morphing into an even greater scene by explaining to Cat that *gross* isn't *disgusting*. In German it means *big* and T.G. had only called her his big sister. That calmed Cat down but T.G. was still pissed at being called an infant. Dad told him to get over it.

I was amused that he spoke in German, the language that he was sure he was going to hate. It kind of gives me hope that he'll learn to like Basti too.

After that, Cat turned to me and gushed, *"Ellen, mon chérie!"*

Give me a break! However, I just said, "Welcome home, Cat."

Over the next few days, I almost feel like the big sister because Cat relies on me to help her navigate our new city. My German isn't great but hers is non-existent so it's kind of fun to help her take the tram and shop and stuff. She acts like I'm more of a friend rather than an annoying presence now and that's the best Christmas present.

On Christmas day, Mom announces, "In the spirit of our host country, I'm roasting a goose for Christmas dinner."

T.G. looks wary but soon the aromas of meat juices, onions, apples and spices fill the house and he is soon stuffing his face as usual. In fact, we all enjoy the goose, as well as the apple and sausage stuffing, the red cabbage, potatoes and veggies. My favorite part of the meal is dessert though. I love Christmas cookies and my favorite are the cinnamon stars called *Zimtsterne*. Cat likes them too but, in true Cat self-control, she only eats one. As I reach for my third, I hesitate for a second and glance at my slim sister.

She looks so pretty I feel an inner sigh. Basti will probably drool when he sees her. Then I mentally slap myself. Basti seems to like me for myself and I don't need to starve because I'm not fat and I stay active. Besides, it's Christmas and one more cookie won't destroy me. I enjoy the cinnamon star as I look around the table at the happy familiar faces and I appreciate how lucky I am.

The rest of the holiday break is busy and, with the lack of snow, thoughts of skiing remain in the background for me. Instead, we all go to holiday parties with new friends and some of Dad's colleagues, explore some of the museums, attend a concert, and have a chance to relax more than normal.

On *Silvesterabend* (New Year's Eve), our school friends, Marco and Manon, invite our family to a party. It's in their family's apartment at the hotel that their dad manages. We have a wonderful meal but the best part as far as T.G. and I are concerned are the "good luck for the new year" desserts.

"Tell me what these all mean, " I ask Manon.

She says, "The little pink marzipan 'lucky' pigs are for prosperity and the cake is topped with 'lucky' chimneysweep figures to sweep away the old year."

"What about the red and white spotted marzipan mushrooms?"

"Oh they're supposed to be lucky too, Ellen, but I forget why."

"That's okay. I'll take any kind of luck!" As I pick one up to taste it, I hope that Basti and I are lucky enough to get to Mittenwald soon.

A poke in the arm from T.G. brings me back to the party and he says, "C'mon, Ellen, we're all going up to the roof."

High above the city at midnight, we watch fireworks being set off in many different parts Munich, accompanied by a chorus of bells ringing in church towers all over the city. We wish one another, *"Einen guten Rutsch!"* — a good slide into the new year. While the adults toast with a bubbly German wine called Sekt, we kids amuse ourselves by heating small balls of *das Bleigießen* in special spoons. We pour the molten lead into cold water and shapes are formed. Then we figure out what the shape looks like and, with the help of a paper that tells us what different shapes mean, we predict what fortune the new year might bring for us. Mine looks like a candle. The directions that came with the spoon and lead say that it means: "Like a light in the darkness, someone will be at your side who is very fond of you. You can rely on this." I think of Basti, smile to myself and wonder if we'll solve this mystery together.

****

It isn't until mid-January that Basti says, "There's good snow in the mountains now, Ellen Troy. I think it's time to ask my parents about inviting you to ski with us."

Without waiting for my reaction, he grabs my hand and says, *"Komm mit."*

"Where to, Basti?"

"To my house. My parents are both home so the timing is perfect!"

"Don't you think you should ask them by yourself? If they don't want to do it, it might be embarrassing for them to say so with me there."

"Kein problem. It will be good for them to see you are interested, no?"

My stomach feels a bit wobbly at this point but I'm not sure if it's from fear of rejection or the fact that Basti is holding my hand. I decide to go along with him.

His parents are both sitting in comfy chairs and reading when we enter their living room. They are quick to flash welcoming smiles when Basti says, *"Hallo, Mutti! Hallo, Poppi!"*

Then his dad says, *"Ah, Ellen, wilkommen!"*
"Danke schön, Herr Hofstetter."

Then his mom says something to me that I don't understand. When I look at Basti for translation, he smiles and tells me that she said I look pretty today. I feel my body sway a bit but I manage to look away from him and turn back to his mom and thank her — all the while hyper-aware that *he's still holding my hand!*

When Basti starts the ski conversation, I'm barely listening, not that it matters. It's all in German so I only understand bits and pieces. I'm pretty sure it's okay with them when I hear his dad say, "Yah!"

However, I soon sense that something else is up and I'm right because Basti switches to English to fill me in.

"Ellen, they want to invite your whole family."

"Really? That's so nice! But why do I get the feeling you don't think so?"

"Na jah, it is nice but your brother will hate it for sure and I don't want to tell them that."

"Then don't. Let my family figure that out. The important thing is that you and I will get to have our time there. Now will you please tell your parents that I think they're very nice to include my family?"

He does and his parents seem pleased. *Yay!* Then Basti suggests Mittenwald, Germany and one minor hitch almost develops when I hear his parents say, *"No. Seefeld, ist besser."*

My own heart skips a beat when I see the panicked look on Basti's face and hear his fast-talking. His parents seem confused by his passionate desire for one town. They ask a lot of questions and I'm dying to understand what reasons Basti is giving. I just hope he isn't revealing the real reason. I'm not sure how they'd react to their son believing in my intuition. I relax when his dad sighs and says, *"Yah gut, Mittenwald."*

As we walk over to my house, I ask Basti what he said to convince them. He said that he told them a lot of things.

"Like what?"

He must sense the tension in my voice because he's quick to say, "Not the real reason."

Phew! "So what unreal reasons did you give?"

"Well the only one that matters is the one that worked."

"Which is?"

"I told them that you love art and I promised to show you a German town with beautiful art on its buildings."

"But that's not true!!"

"No, but it's only a small lie. Mittenwald has beautiful painted buildings and I think you do like art."

"Why?"

"Your mama is a painter and your papa finds ancient art treasures, no? Art is a big part of your world, I think."

It pretty much leaves me speechless that Basti thinks about what I like — even if it is part of a cover-up.

When we go to my dad and mom, they're delighted with the offer and agree for the following Saturday. T.G., as predicted, balks at the idea when Mom and Dad mention it at dinner. The thought of Basti giving him pointers is painful. He only says yes when Dad assures him that he may join a ski class for the day.

During midweek, Basti promises me that he will research the address for the Schillers who took care of Helmut Koch during the war and it turns out to be pretty simple. The best part is that *Haus* Schiller is located close to one of the beginner ski lifts. We hope it will be easy to slip away for a bit without arousing parental suspicion.

****

Saturday dawns cold and clear. It's torture to get up early but, once we're on the highway, Dad says he's glad that we left as early as *Herr* Hofstetter suggested.

The *Garmischer Autobahn* is crowded with mountain-bound vacationers, even at 7 am, and we're told that it will get worse as the morning progresses. Despite his years of driving in free-spirited Italy, Dad is still not used to the speed on the German highways and his attempts to follow the Hofstetter car amount to white-knuckle driving. We're all relieved when we pull into the parking lot at Mittenwald.

When we arrive at the mountain, *Herr* Hofstetter suggests that his wife and kids head out and take a few runs while he helps us rent equipment and join ski classes. Then he'll call their cell phone to find out where to meet. (At least that's what I think he said, given my beginner German level.)

Frau Hofstetter agrees and then wishes us, *"Viel Glück!"*

Dad laughs and says, "It will take some luck for me not to fall!"

As Basti is leaving, he leans his head in and whispers, *"Bis später*, Ellen Troy."

I smile because *later* hopefully means finding the Schillers.

Once the others are off, my family follows *Herr* Hofstetter to the rental place. When we're all organized, he asks Dad, *"Mittagessen um halb zwölf Uhr?"*

Dad's face scrunches up, as if to say, *Say what?* and he asks, *"Bitte?"*

Herr Hofstetter thinks for a minute and then says "Mittagessen... lunch, no?" and then he mimes eating.

Dad smiles and says, "Lunch! Yes! What time... uh, *Uhr?"*

Herr Hofstetter holds up 10 fingers, then 2 and says, *"Zwölf."*

"Twelve," Dad answers.

Then *Herr* Hofstetter adds, *"Und ein halb."*

Dad looks blank again but I come to his rescue and tell him, "Twelve and a half, Dad. You know, twelve-thirty."

A light bulb seems to dawn and he smiles again, looks at *Herr* Hofstetter and says, *"Zwölf und ein halb. Gut."*

They shake hands and both seem relieved. Communication is hard work sometimes.

After some shaky starts when we get outside, Dad and Mom are making decent snowplow moves, learning how to fall (with frequency) and, despite exhausting themselves, seem to be having fun. When Dad face plants, T.G. yells, "Nice one, Dad!"

"Hah! Just you wait, Alexander, I'll be racing you down the slopes before you know it!"

Judging from the way my athletic and motivated brother is moving through the learning curve with ease, I seriously doubt it, but I yell, "Go, Dad!"

Dad laughs and says, "I'll be racing you too, Ellen!"

As if either one of us is going to be racing any time soon. I'm precise but cautious. I've mastered the snowplow and I'm beginning to maneuver some slow parallel turns, but it will be a long process.

By the time lunch comes, we're all famished and head into the lodge to meet the Hofstetters for lunch.

Basti suggests, "Try the *Gulaschsuppe*, Ellen Troy. It's good after skiing."

I do and he's right; it's tastes like spicy beef stew and it warms me right up. "This is good, Basti. I like it."

With a tease in his voice, he asks, "Is it yummy?"

I laugh and say, "Yes it is yummy. You remember funny English words very well."

When everyone is finished eating, *Herr* Hofstetter speaks to his son and Basti translates for us.

"Papa says that, if you want to go back out on the practice hill, our family will come along and help you."

Dad looks at Mom and asks, "How do you feel Carolina? My muscles are a bit sore but I'm game to go out for a little while longer, if you are."

Mom says, "I may regret it tomorrow but I'd like to try some more. How about you kids?"

Basti and I lock eyes. We know that this is our only chance to see the Schillers and we have to get away from the group. Before we can say anything, however, T.G. asks, "Please let me take another lesson? I was on a roll out there and I want to keep the momentum going."

Dad and Mom look at each other and seem to reach some silent agreement before Dad says, "I suppose that will be okay. Do you want another lesson as well, Ellen?"

I shake my head and then Dad asks Basti to explain about T.G. to his parents. He does and *Herr* Hofstetter offers to help again. As the three of them get ready to head to the ski school, *Herr* Hofstetter says that he and Dad will meet the rest of us outside where we left our skis.

Basti grabs the opportunity and tells them that the two of us would like to ski by ourselves.

Dad is quick to say, "Ellen, you're just learning. You can't keep up with Basti."

I don't know what to say but Basti comes to my rescue. "Not to worry, Mr. Madigan. We will ski only on the easy hill and I will help her."

Then his papa says something about time and Basti promises that we will meet them at 16:00 at the car. He still seems unconvinced but his wife whispers something in his ear and he sighs. He looks at my parents and asks, *"Zoh?"*

Dad grimaces but Mom says, "Oh, Andrew, they'll be fine."

Finally, Dad nods at *Herr* Hofstetter and Basti and I breathe a sigh of relief.

Before our parents can change their minds, we're out the door. We grab our skis and head for the easy slope closest to *Haus* Schiller. After two runs with Basti staying close to my cautious pace, we stash our skis on a rack and take off in search of the house, slowed only by our clunky ski boots.

As we trudge through the town I tell Basti, "Mittenwald looks to me like a storybook alpine village."

"And do you like the art on the buildings, Ellen Troy?"

"Of course, Basti. I love art, just like you told your parents."

He stops, looks into my eyes and says, "What else do you love, Ellen Troy?"

I love that his eyes are a soft brown with glints of gold that seem to touch my soul, but I can't say it. I struggle for

the right words that won't leave me too vulnerable and settle
on, "I love that you trust me enough to bring me here, Basti."

He seems good with that and he takes my hand as
we continue. We find the house tucked into a narrow street
amidst shops selling goods that are handcrafted on the
premises. An elderly woman, dressed in the traditional dirndl
dress, answers our knock on the door. We're relieved when
she answers to the name of *Frau* Schiller, the same one who
had cared for the young Helmut Koch. Basti makes a quick
explanation of the reason for our visit and she invites us to
come inside. As we take off our boots, she calls for her
husband to join us, *"Oskar, komm schon!"*

When we sit down with the both of them, Basti asks
the questions in German and translates into English for me.
His first question is, "Do you remember two women called
Liesi and Magda?"

Frau Schiller says, "Yah, they worked with *Doktor*
Grüber."

"Did Liesi and Magda come to you when they were
fleeing the Nazis?"

Her body stiffens and her face loses its color as she
answers, *"Nein.* They only brought us children, like Helmut
Koch. Beyond that, we asked no questions. It was safer that
way."

Herr Schiller, who has been silent up to now, adds,
"There is one thing I know, however. *Doktor* Grüber worked

with a network of other families. He revealed that to us out of necessity through Liesi and Magda. They brought us a sealed envelope with emergency instructions to be used in case anything ever happened to him. For everyone's protection, they insisted that we hide it under a floorboard and open it only if necessary."

Basti's voice seems hopeful as he asks, "Is that envelope still hidden here?"

Herr Schiller replies, *"Nein."*

Basti and I feel disappointed but then *Herr* Schiller continues, "During the war, it was wise to leave nothing in writing that could be incriminating. We opened the envelope, memorized its contents and burnt the paper. The safest notation was in one's head."

With a mounting sense of excitement, Basti asks, "Do you remember what it said, *Herr* Schiller?"

"Hah! I may be old, but my memory is still good. There were six names of people who helped *Doktor* Grüber and I memorized them! Would you like to hear them?"

Duh!

By the time we leave *Haus* Schiller, it's almost 15:30. We have time to take two more runs before meeting our parents in the parking lot. When asked if we had a good afternoon, we say that it has been *fantastisch*.

Chapter 15 — The List

It isn't until the following Thursday that Basti and I have time to focus on the list. We meet at the bus stop after school and go into the public library in Arabellapark. He removes the scribbled notes from his jacket pocket, and then we look at the list together. Five are in Austria: Ernst Kneller in Seefeld, Claus Görlitz in Telfs, Gerhard Meissner in Imst, Karl Dollmann in Landeck, and Wolfgang Herderer in Ischgl. The sixth one is Johann König in Samnaun, Switzerland. I'm guessing that similar thoughts are running through each of our minds; will any of them remember Liesi and Magda, and are any of them still alive?

Moving into action, Basti starts a computer search. While he types, I think back to the memory trick *Herr* Schiller described to us. It had served him well even after all this time. He had made up two sentences about transporting children to safety as a way to remember. In the first sentence, he made the first letter of each man's last name the first letter of each word in the sentence.

KGMDHK

Kinder Gehen Mit Dem Herzlichen Kerle

(Children go with sincere fellows.)

In the second sentence, he did the same thing with the first letter of each town.

STILIS

Sicherheit Transport Im Land Ist Schwer.

(Safety transport in the country is difficult.)

As for the men's' first names, he had relied on memory for those. He claimed that, once he had the last names, the first were no problem. I think it's amazing; the man must have a photographic memory!

I turn from my thoughts to watch over Basti's shoulder as he scrolls German websites. After about twenty minutes of searching, he says, "Okay, that's it! Two of the men are located — Kneller in Seefeld and König in Samnaun."

I write down the addresses and telephone numbers and then, realizing that it's getting late, we head for home. Before parting, we agree that another ski trip or two is called for since both Seefeld and Samnaun are ski areas.

Basti tells me, "Seefeld, Austria is a short drive over the border from Mittenwald so we should focus on Kneller first."

I agree and, individually, we lobby our parents for another ski trip. Two weeks later we're all headed for Seefeld in the early Saturday morning hours.

Basti and I use the same scenario as in Mittenwald. He skis with his family while I take a morning lesson and then we go off on our own after lunch. This time, however, we don't take a couple of runs before seeking out *Herr* Kneller. He lives in the valley about a mile from the ski lifts so there's not much time. It's way too far to walk in our ski boots but we're prepared. As we leave the lodge, Basti grabs his backpack that has our shoes in it. Out of sight of our parents, we switch our boots for the shoes, stow the backpack in a safe place and set out to find *Herr* Kneller.

An elderly guy, dressed in woolen pants and a traditional gray sweater with silver buttons and red and green trim, greets us at the door. His cheeks are the pink of an outdoorsman and his silver hair is long behind his ears. *Herr* Kneller listens without emotion to Basti's story and then seems to evaluate the two of us before opening the door wide enough for us to enter.

"Please excuse the clutter. I lost my wife a few years ago and, now that I'm alone, I am not so fussy."

There is no clutter, except for a few books and newspapers on the table and he removes those as he says, "Please have a seat."

He rummages around in the cupboards, making small talk as he does. He says he will make us all some hot chocolate because we must be cold after our walk. He too needs to warm up because he has just come in from cross-country skiing. "I'm no longer much good at downhill skiing but I'm still strong enough for *Langlaufen*," he boasts.

When the steaming mugs are placed in front of us, *Herr* Kneller says that he remembers the two young women well and he begins to reminisce. "They delivered at least a dozen children to me during the war. The last time I saw them however, was when *Doktor* Söllbach delivered the women themselves. He had smuggled them across the border into Austria at Scharnitz in a hay truck, after Liesi's wounds seemed to be mending. I sheltered them overnight in my own barn and fed them."

Basti interrupts to say, "I thank you for my family, *Herr* Kneller."

"It was simply the right thing to do, young man. Afterwards, I delivered them the following day to *Herr* Görlitz in Telfs, a town further south. They were supposed to continue this pattern of hayrides until they reached the alpine town of Ischgl, Austria where arrangements had been made through the underground network for new identity papers. The goal was for them to hike over a peak from Austria into neutral Switzerland at Samnaun."

"Do you know if they made it there, *Herr* Kneller?"

"I hoped things went well for them but I never heard if they made it."

Grasping onto the Samnaun connection, we thank him for the information and the hot chocolate and begin the trek back across the snow feeling hopeful. As we walk and talk, we both agree that there are still a lot of "ifs" — *If Herr* König is still alive…*if* the women had connected with him…*if* we ourselves can get to Switzerland. We need all of these things to work out and it seems a lot to hope for.

Chapter 16 — Ski Week

"Wahnsinnig!" Basti's reaction to my news mystifies me at first. "Why is the Munich International School family ski week in Galtür, Austria *crazy*?"

"It is fate, don't you see, Ellen Troy?"

I don't see it at all. I've never even heard of Galtür. How am I supposed to have an opinion about it?

Looking at my confused expression with amusement, he explains, "Galtür is part of the Silvretta mountains in Austria, and the Silvretta ski pass is good for several connecting areas. Galtür connects to Ischgl and Ischgl connects to... Samnaun, Switzerland!"

The importance of his words hit me. "It *is* fate! I'm meant to be there. So... all I have to do is ski over the pass into Switzerland and talk to *Herr* König... Hah! Like that's gonna happen. No way. I'm a beginner skier and I'm just learning German. You have to do this, Basti. I'll just have to get my family to invite you along for the week."

"I can't, Ellen. I have school that week and my parents will never let me miss that much time. Plus, it would be too hard to catch up."

So I will have to go it alone. As if.

The two of us walk along in silence until Basti suggests an alternative. "The ski terrain over the pass is beyond your abilities, Ellen Troy, but if you take the ski lift in Ischgl to the top of the peak, you can then ride another lift down into Samnaun. If you're willing to do that, I will write a letter for you in German to give to *Herr* König."

"It seems a bit daunting."

"But it may be our only chance to talk to the man in person — at least in the near future!"

"Well, what if I can get my friend, Manon Van Hoorn, to go with me, Basti? She'll be on the school trip, speaks fluent German and I trust her."

"That might work. Ask her and, in the meantime, I'll work on the letter."

As promised, he gives it to me before I leave.

****

We Madigans drive into the long snow-covered valley on a Saturday morning in late February. As we pass through the town of Ischgl, I'm a bit overwhelmed by the sight of the massive peaks decked with ski lifts traveling in all directions. Continuing into Galtür, my apprehension increases as the network of lifts continues and the elevation rises. How will I ever find my way to the correct lift?

It isn't until several days and several lessons later that I begin to feel comfortable enough reading the trail maps and I think of my mission.

I decide to ask Manon for help after dinner at our hotel. Tonight, a group of us are watching a film together and I make a point of sitting next to Manon. We haven't seen much of each other during the days because I've been busy with lessons and Manon, who is an excellent skier, has spent her days on more challenging terrain with Marco and a group of their friends. I know that asking Manon to spend a good part of the day going off with a beginner like myself is asking a lot but I plunge ahead anyway. In a whisper, so as not to disturb the others listening to the film, I ask, "Manon, have you been over to Samnaun yet?"

Her answer is, "I haven't but it's one of the things I'd like to do before the week is up. I'm having trouble convincing Marco and the others to go with me because they say that they have plenty of variety here. They don't see the need to venture so far, just to say that they have skied into another country. Some people just aren't adventurous!"

I couldn't have hoped for a better opening. "I need to go to Samnaun, Manon."

"What do you mean you *need* to go?"

I swallow hard because I know that I'm opening myself up to more questions than I want to answer. I need an ally so I explain. "I promised my friend Basti that I would get an important message to someone in Samnaun. I need someone who speaks German to help out... I wouldn't ask you if it wasn't so important."

"It sounds cool but that trail on the Swiss side isn't groomed and we might have to ski through deep snow. I'm not sure you can handle it yet..."

I concede that it's true and I tell her what Basti suggested. Manon agrees that it makes sense... for me, but for her, the whole point of going is to enjoy the deep snow!

She thinks for a minute and then suggests, "How about you take the lift down and I meet you at the bottom?"

"That's fine," I say, "as long as you agree to one more thing. It's okay to tell people that we're going to Samnaun but please don't tell anyone *why* we're going."

"No problem," she says and the deal is made for the next day.

****

In the morning, I go to my lesson but I leave the group early to meet Manon at 11 am as planned. Rather than make our way over to Ischgl on skis, which will take too long at my pace, we hop on the local bus. It deposits us near the base of the lift we need to take and we're soon being conveyed upward toward the ridge that is part of the border between Austria and Switzerland. At the summit, we part ways and agree to meet at the base of the lift in Samnaun. I watch as Manon disappears down the mountain and around a bend with ease, leaving a trail of spraying snow in her wake. Then I push myself along to the top of the Swiss lift and I board it for its return to the bottom

As I wait at the base for Manon, I'm struck by the contrast from the less commercial Austrian side. Samnaun, Switzerland is filled not only with inns and restaurants but also with lots of touristy shops selling duty-free items like perfume, whiskey and chocolate. Catering to Austrian day-trippers looking for a tax break seems to be a popular business.

Manon soon arrives in a state of near exhilaration. "The snow was so deep and mostly untracked — like virgin territory!" she exclaims. "I saw hardly any other skiers, which is amazing considering how bustling the town seems to be."

My own method of transportation riding the ski lift seems to be the day-trippers' choice.

We lock up our skis and then I show Manon the address Basti wrote on the envelope. She asks a local for directions and then we head into the labyrinth of the village.

After a slow trek in our ski boots, we find the house. It's imposing and quite large. As we start up the walk, Manon nudges me. *"Schau mal auf die Alpendohle!"* Reacting to my quizzical expression, she points and switches to English. "Look at the crow!"

A large bluish-black bird is standing before the doorway and watching our approach. Undaunted, we start up the steps but the crow opens its beak and caws loud enough to startle us into a retreat.

Crowing of a human sort then catches our attention and we turn to be confronted by a birdlike old woman clutching a small dog. In a mountain dialect similar to Bavarian, she wants to know what business we have there.

Manon explains that we're looking for *Herr* Johann König.

The old woman cackles in a humorless way and says, *"Zu spat"* which I know means *too late*. Glancing at the bird, she continues talking but the only thing I can pick up from her words is *Sankt Jakob*.

Manon then asks her a question about *Sankt Jacob*. I don't understand much of the question or answer but Manon whispers that the old woman is talking in riddles!

I can hear the frustration in Manon's voice as she asks another question and then I notice her eyes widen. She turns to me and says, "She said to follow the crow!"

The words are barely out of her mouth when the fluttering of wings causes our heads to turn. We watch as the bird takes off and, when we turn back, the woman has disappeared.

Manon says, "That old woman is batty!"

I shake my head. "No, she's right. We have to find *Sankt Jakob* and the crow. I have a feeling it's important."

Manon looks at me like she thinks I'm also a little batty but she says nothing and follows my lead. I'm determined and I even use my shaky German to ask a passerby the way to *Sankt Jakob*. A short while later, we find ourselves in front of a church. Strange. Why would he go to a church and not go home again? The only way to find out is to go inside. The church is quiet and nearly empty but we spot a priest toward the front and head in his direction. Manon explains our quest and he escorts us to the side door and says that *Herr* König is outside.

The cold winter air merely nips at our noses but the sight before us chills our bones. It's a cemetery. The priest directs us to the far corner, where we find the final resting-place for *Herr* Johann König and his wife Helga. It is, in more ways than one, a dead end and I feel discouraged. I realize that Basti and I may never find out what happened to Liesi. I stare at the grave marker and wonder why my intuition has led me here. He died in 1995 at the age of eighty, and his wife died before that. They can't answer any of my questions now.

When I hear the fluttering of wings, I know before I look that it will be the crow. It whooshes by our heads but it doesn't stop at the König marker. It flies in a circle above the graveyard and then lands several rows over. Without speaking, we follow the bird and find it perched atop another grave marker. The inscription reads *Gisela von Werz*. The name in itself means nothing to me but the date *1920–1946* is more interesting. Liesi Falke and Magda Alt would have arrived in Samnaun toward the end of 1943 and they would have been the same age as Gisela. Interesting, yes… but what does it really mean?

I grab Manon by the arm and, as we walk back toward the church, I tell her what I need her to do. At this point,

Manon seems to sense that something important is happening and she agrees to ask the priest about the woman whose name is on the headstone.

He's too young to remember her but he does recall that *Herr* König and his wife had sometimes brought flowers to her grave. One day out of curiosity, he had asked them if she was a relative. The old man had hesitated but then smiled at his wife and said, "She was a friend whose gift was immeasurable to our lives."

I know that Liesi and Magda were heading for *Herr* König's home after they fled. Is Gisela von Werz another woman entirely or is it a false identity for one of them? We ask if there are any other graves that the Königs visited but his answer is, "No." The priest can shed no more light on the puzzle but it's a tantalizing piece that he provides.

As we head back toward the lift that will return us to Austria, I think about what I have learned. The delivery of Basti's letter may have been aborted but the quest is getting more interesting, and also more complicated. It's just a question of what to do next. I don't ask Manon for advice because I haven't told her about Liesi and Magda. I hope Basti will have an idea. In the meantime, there's no reason that Manon and I can't get ourselves some Swiss chocolate before riding the lift back across the border. We've burned enough calories today to earn a piece. Besides, studies say that the flavonoids in chocolate boost energy and brainpower and I've got a lot of figuring out to do. I love science, especially when it confirms that what tastes good can also be good for me!

****

A furious snowstorm on Saturday makes the drive back to *München* stressful and much longer than normal. Dad and Mom say they feel spent — Dad from the responsibility of steering on slippery roads and Mom from the constant phantom braking she finds herself doing in the front passenger seat. T.G. and I exhaust ourselves by bickering over space in the backseat, about who cheats at card games, which one of us did the best jump over the small mound at the side of the beginner slope, which ski trail was the most challenging, and so on. We probably give our parents a welcome break when we both fall asleep just before crossing the border back into Germany.

When we arrive home, it's already dark and the unpacking of the car is left for the morning by mutual consent. Ski week was fun, but for us beginner skiers, it was very tiring and everyone's happy to go to bed earlier than usual. My news for Basti will have to wait until morning as well.

February 18, 1943 — The Sixth Leaflet

She had been avoiding Magdalena for weeks because she was afraid. She had sensed honesty in her voice but who could be sure now? She also worried that Georg suspected something. Even as her own courage waned, however, it seemed to her that the resistance was escalating. Lately she had seen bold anti-Hitler graffiti on Ludwigstrasse near the Universität. The shame rose within her each time she encountered someone else's bravery and it tortured her that she was afraid to stand up for freedom. She tried to lose herself in her studies but it was an effort and the lecture she was attending that day was particularly dry. When it was over, she roused herself and headed for the door. Entering the atrium that was the central hall of the building, a shower of white papers startled her. Their appearance brought surprised reactions and accelerated the normal noise and confusion as students poured out of the lecture halls. As she looked upwards, one of the papers floated onto her notebook and she sensed what it was before she even looked — the sixth leaflet. Someone pointed toward the upper level. Two figures were standing under an archway that was part of an arcade on the second-floor balcony. She couldn't see their faces because they were in the shadows but they appeared to be observing the flurry of activity. She guessed that they might be the source of the leaflets and she felt a sense of admiration for them. Then one of the university custodians pushed past her muttering something about the Polizei and a sense of panic overtook her. She pushed her way through the crowd and emerged from the building breathless, just moments before the doors were ordered shut. Trembling, she ran through the courtyard toward the main street and stopped only long enough to notice the words "Fellow Fighters in the Resistance!" as she threw her leaflet into a trash barrel.

Her telephone rang later that evening and the sound of Magdalena's quiet voice was a shock. She hadn't identified herself but she knew who she was. The message was quite ordinary but, at the same time, it was urgent. "I found your lecture notes, and I left them with Hansi." That was all she said and then she hung up.

Her mind raced trying to decipher the meaning of the cryptic words. Her notebook hadn't been lost, so she must have been referring to something else…but what? And Hansi… who was Hansi? The only Hansi she could think of was the newsagent in Marienplatz. Was she supposed to go there? It was after curfew so it was too late to be going into the Innenstadt and too risky. The local Nazi party leader, the Gauleiter who monitored activity on her street in the evening, would be sure to question where she was going. What was Magdalena thinking? It would have to wait until morning.

She had no lecture the following morning but she got up early anyway and took the tram to Marienplatz. Hansi was there but he expressed bewilderment when she asked about a notebook. Murmuring that she must have misunderstood, she was about to turn away when a thought struck her and she fished in her pocket for a coin to purchase a newspaper. She made her way over to the side of the Platz and leaned against a building as she scanned the pages.

The news was devastating. Her classmate, Hans Scholl, and his sister Sophie had been arrested for distributing the leaflets! She knew that Hans had a number of close friends who were also in the medical program — Alex Schmorell, Jurgen Wittenstein, Christoph Probst and Willi Graf, and now she feared for them as well. Who knew that such daring individuals had inhabited the same lecture halls that she did? She felt in awe of them but also diminished by her own cowardice.

She rolled up the paper and started to walk toward the tram when it hit her. Hansi! Perhaps Magdalena had been trying to tell her about Hans Scholl! But what about her lecture notes? That made no sense. There were no lecture notes to give Hans... unless she had given him something else...like...like...like the fact that she was sympathetic to their cause? Oh God! Now she was really scared. What if her name had been written down? A feeling of nausea overcame *her, and her hands felt clammy. She tried to control her breathing and think clearly. She decided that she would just have to try and act normal in case her actions were being watched. As much as she dreaded going near the Universität, she would force herself to attend her afternoon lecture and pretend that the previous day's events had meant nothing to her personally.*

Chapter 17 — The Next Step

I'm awake early the next morning, trembling from yet another vivid dream. The woman's fear of arrest at the hands of the brutal Nazis was clear and I'm reminded of Liesi's fearful diary entries. It has to be about her but, then again, fear was everywhere during that time. It's so frustrating. I'm getting bits and pieces of puzzles but I need more to figure out what I'm meant to do. I let out a sigh as I give up trying to sleep any longer and put down the details in my diary. I also update Basti's family tree again with another question mark — could Gisela be Liesi?

Christoph and Sigrid Falke
great, great grandparents (built Haus Falke)

Dr. Anna (Falke) Schumann   *Elizabeth Falke*
great grandma (Uroma)   *(Liesi) - (survived?)*
                                        (Gisela?)

Dr. Sabine Müller
grandma (Oma)

Silke Hofstetter (m. Franz)
Parents

Sebastian (Basti) & Annika

Realizing that the others are still sound asleep, I slip into some clothes, tiptoe downstairs, and make myself some hot chocolate. I'm anxious to see Basti but I don't want to annoy his family by waking everyone up too early. So I sip my chocolate and bide my time. When I can't wait any longer, I grab a jacket and head outside. Perhaps I will be able to tell if they're up if I walk past the front of their house.

The air is cold and I can see my breath. I soon regret not putting on a hat but don't feel like going back for one. As I stroll past *Haus* Schumann, I see that the house is still dark. With my head tucked down into my jacket collar, I turn around and head back. Absorbed with my thoughts, I walk right into someone in my path. Startled, I make a muffled apology, *"Es tut mir leid!"*

The person doesn't move and the eyes that meet mine when I glance up are smiling. Basti hugs me and touches my ice-cold nose. "It's been a long week, Ellen Troy."

Suddenly it doesn't seem so cold out any more. Does this mean that he missed me? I hope so but I can't bring myself to ask. Instead, I struggle to sound matter-of-fact and just say, "Yes, I've been anxious to tell you what happened. You see…"

"Not here. You're practically frozen."

Conceding that it's true, I offer to make us both some breakfast. Basti points out that it will be hard to discuss my Swiss visit if my parents are there. "How about letting me buy you breakfast at Café Wiedemann? It's in the neighborhood."

That sounds like a better idea so I run back to the house to leave a note on the kitchen table for my parents. Then I grab a hat and gloves as I head out the door once again.

Several blocks later, we arrive at the café and its cozy warmth, combined with the chill-chasing heat of our food, feels good. We settle into a booth by a window and, though the wintry scene outside is pretty, my focus is on telling Basti about Samnaun. He is soon riveted by my recounting of the Swiss adventure.

When I'm done, he gazes through the frosted sunlit window trying to process the information. When he does speak, he questions me. "Could it really be Liesi or Magda in a grave marked Gisela von Werz in a small church cemetery in the Swiss mountains? I think it is a very long shot at best, Ellen Troy."

He searches my face for signs of doubt and, when he sees none, makes his case. "As I see it, there are many problems. If one of the women is this Gisela, how can we know for sure? It seems that all of the witnesses are dead or missing. If one or both of them survived, why wouldn't they return to their families in *München*? Then again, if one or both survived, and for some reason couldn't return, where would they go? My guess is that they would have stayed in a German-speaking country — perhaps another town in Switzerland, or they returned to Germany or went to Austria? That would mean that we have at least three countries to search. As for the names, would we search for their old identities or their wartime ones? To complicate matters, we don't know their wartime identities nor do we know if they may have married and taken a husband's surname. Plus, there are so many unknown possibilities. One or both might still be alive but, then again, they could be dead. We might need to search millions of employment records, telephone books, marriage, death, and even emigration records. It is, as we say in German, *'Eher geht ein Kamel durchs Nadelöhr'."*

"What does that mean?"

Basti sighs and says, "It means that it's easier for a camel to go through the eye of a needle."

"Oh, I get it. It's kind of like us saying it's like searching for a needle in a haystack."

"Ah zoh. Either way it would require the resources of several governments. We're just two teenagers, Ellen Troy. We can't track them down with a few coins and a telephone this time."

For a few moments, the silence is almost deafening. I realize that it's time to go for broke and test his confidence in my ability. "Basti, do you believe that I was drawn to her story by accident? I felt the pull of it the first time I entered *Haus* Falke! I felt the need to learn more when I stood over the old foundation in the basement! It led you to read me her diary and that helped us find the clues to her trail and the people she encountered. Even Manon realized that the crow in Samnaun was guiding us! Gisela von Werz can't be a dead end. She has to be a continuation of this journey. I don't know how we're going to find out about her but I know that we must."

I see that my fire has unnerved him a bit and I prepare myself for his reaction. When it comes, I'm surprised. "From the moment you took me down into the basement, Ellen Troy, I feel like I am pulled into a strong sea. It is *comisch* but I do not fight it and I have no fear. You guide me like a *fantastisch* sea creature and I trust you will not let me go under. I think only that you take me to a new place and I will learn new things."

He has just bowled me over. He trusts me and I'm tempted to tell him about the dreams but all I say is, "I hope we'll get to that knowledge together, Basti."

"What do you suggest we do first then, Ellen Troy?"

My answer is a bit lame. "Honestly Basti, I don't know. I guess we'll just have to hope that something continues to guide us."

Chapter 18 — Seeking the "Needle in the Haystack"

Mid-March in *München* is still cold and gray but splashes of colored Easter eggs poke through the dullness. There are yellow, pink, blue, purple and green decorated wooden ones in the craft shops, dyed hard-cooked red ones in the markets, and marzipan and foil-wrapped chocolate ones in the sweet shops. They announce the coming of spring and sunnier days ahead, and Basti and I are hoping for better days.

This Saturday morning, we're downtown in the *Füssgänger* zone and all along the walkway are wooden stands selling costumes, masks, confetti and noisemakers. It's the pre-Lent Mardi Gras time that the Germans call *Fasching* and shops are selling *Krapfen*, the traditional jelly doughnuts of the season.

"Oh look, Basti," I yell. "Some people are in costume!"

"*Na jah*, they are still making their way home from last evening's parties. There are costume balls all over the city on the weekends and they have many themes — the classical ball, the jungle ball, the ball of 1,000 fancy cakes, one where everyone must wear white and even one where you are supposed to wear as little as you dare!"

"Oh I know about the balls! My parents went to one last week where every woman was given a large pink plastic umbrella as a favor."

"Yah, for sure it's a season of silliness!"

I've come downtown to find a mask to wear to the Middle School's *Fasching* dance and Basti needs one for an event of his own. However, it's hard to think about having fun. It's been almost three weeks since I returned from Samnaun and I've experienced no new "feelings" and haven't seen any prophetic crows. The main reason we're together today is to plan our next move but the day ends without any ideas.

As the days progress, Basti and I come to the conclusion that we have to make some sort of start, no matter how feeble. Meeting after school one day, he suggests, "Let's go to the public library computers and write letters to the German, Austrian and Swiss bureaus of records, Ellen Troy."

"Good idea, but *you'll* have to actually write the messages in German. I'll help with ideas."

In the letters we ask for advice on how to track down missing war refugees. After mailing them, we have little to do but get on with our lives and hope for the best.

Throughout April and May, Basti and I are kept busy with school demands. Although trees bud and flowers bloom, the spring brings no rebirth of hope for our quest. We receive no answers to our letters so our lives revolve around other things... until one special day in June.

When I wake up on June 4th, I'm greeted by blazing sunshine. I smile to myself and then I address the solar orb. "Thank you for providing such a glorious start to *my* day!" I accept it as a personal gift because it *is* my special day — my fifteenth birthday.

Enjoying the Saturday morning luxury of staying in bed, I lie there for a bit reflecting on my life. I've had a good beginning so far but I'm determined to use my increasing maturity to make things happen, have an impact and leave my unique mark on the world. I'm full of hopes and dreams and I have good vibes about the upcoming year. Something will happen. I can *feel* it!

In a good mood, I leap from my bed and head downstairs to the kitchen, expecting my presents to be arranged on my breakfast plate like every year before. However, there are no presents and no plate. The place is deserted — no Mom, no Dad, no T.G. I can't believe that they haven't even left me a card! Tears begin to well up in my eyes and then I see the note propped against the toaster.

Happy Birthday Ellen!

 Thought we'd let you sleep on this special day rather than wake you to come grocery shopping with us so early. We may also stop at the large flea market on the east side of the city that we've heard so much about. So... we probably won't return until late afternoon. If you decide to go out, just leave a note regarding your plans so we won't worry.

 Enjoy this beautiful day!

 Love, Mom and Dad

I can't believe it! I *absotively posolutely* can't believe it! It's my fifteenth freakin' birthday and my own parents have told me to have fun all by myself! My lips begin to quiver and the tears that have been poised in the rims of my eyes overflow the fleshy dams and trickle down my cheeks. The ringing of the doorbell seems like a gloomy song that only emphasizes my sadness. I'm tempted to ignore it but when I hear Basti's voice, I push myself toward the door, wiping my cheeks as I go.

"Hey, are you all right, Ellen Troy? You look a little off." Seeming a bit uncomfortable by my appearance, he averts his eyes and heads for the kitchen as he often does on a Saturday morning. He calls to me over his shoulder as he walks. "It's too nice a day to still be in your pajamas, Ellen Troy. Go upstairs and get dressed while I have some juice or something. It's a day for adventure in the city, *gelt?*"

It's all too much for me — yet another person who should know it's my birthday and is blowing it off! Taking the stairs two at a time, I race back to my room, throw myself onto the bed, and have a good cry. After several minutes of wallowing, I glance at the clock. It's nearing ten and my day will slip away fast if I don't get moving. Despite them all, I'm going to make this day memorable. With a new determination, I head into the shower to wash away my gloom.

The "me" that enters the kitchen twenty minutes later has a fresh-scrubbed look and a set smile on her face. "I'm ready for adventure, but I think I need to do it alone today."

I can see that this statement stuns Basti. "Are you telling me to go away?"

"No offense, but I guess I am."

"At least tell me where you're going?"

A thought occurs to me, and I ignore his question and look for a piece of paper. I need to leave my parents a note.

Mom and Dad,

Went to see about renting a
horse for a ride in the Englischer
Garten. Then I might buy myself
lunch at the Seehaus and watch the
paddleboats in the lake. Happy
Birthday to me!

Your fifteen-year-old daughter,

Ellen

Thrusting the note down on the table, I glare at Basti, tell him to lock the door after he leaves and bolt out the door.

I make my way to the riding complex run by *SportScheck*, a large sport department store in the city. The stables are near the *Englischer Garten* at Unterföhring and I'm able to rent a horse there. The horseback ride through the curved paths of the park cheers me up some, even if I do cry so much that the scenery is blurry.

Afterwards, the *Seehaus* is crowded and I share an outdoor table with several welcoming strangers who have their dogs sitting at their feet. Even so, I feel miserable and alone.

I'm mindlessly pushing food around my plate and staring out at the lake when Dad finds me. He barks words at me, and doesn't even give me a chance to respond. "Ellen Theodora Madigan, what were you thinking? Who gave you permission to go horseback riding alone? You could have been hurt! I'm just glad that I can bring you to your mother in one piece! She's waiting for us just a few blocks away so let's go!"

I'm confused and hurt by his reaction because he knows full well that I learned to ride safely when I was a kid. However, I stumble up from the table and follow him just the same. Feeling miserable, I say nothing as we head out of the park on the west side and into a side street of the Schwabing area. As we turn the corner onto Leopoldstrasse, Schwabing's main boulevard, I ask where we're meeting Mom.

His answer is vague. "She's waiting in a place just a bit further ahead."

Before long, he's guiding me into an ice cream shop. As we make our way past occupied tables, I stop. At the very last one is Mom but she isn't alone. Around her, sporting huge grins, are T.G., Basti, Manon and Marco. A huge cluster of balloons is attached to an empty chair, and a pile of wrapped packages clutters the table. A chorus of 'Happy Birthday starts and, once again, I begin to cry — this time from happiness!

Mom hugs me and laughs. "You certainly made this difficult, honey. Basti was supposed to be in charge of getting you here on time but you ran out on him!"

"I guess I just thought you all forgot so I wanted to be alone — but no matter, as far as I'm concerned, my real birthday is starting now."

When they all begin to clap, I turn to see a huge frozen ice cream concoction lit with sparklers being carried to our table. As the flickering lights peter out, I'm amazed to see that it's big enough to feed all of us from one huge bowl!

The time flies by and I receive many memorable gifts. The most special by far, however, is from Basti. It's a locket that his *Uroma*, Anna, gave to him and it belonged to Liesi. As I pick it up, I feel good vibrations and sense that we just might not need to wait for any letters.

Chapter 19 — The Locket

I wait until I'm alone in my room to open the locket. I sense that there will be a photo of Liesi or of someone close to her but I don't know for sure. I doubt that Basti would have put in his own photo, but just in case, I didn't want to invite any teasing from T.G. or the others. Basti and I are friends — no big deal, right?

I dangle the oval from its chain and hold it up to better observe it. The vintage silver is slightly worn and the front of it is engraved with the words *Gott schutze dich* surrounded by raised curly patterns. I know that the words mean *God protect you* and I can't help but think that maybe Liesi should have worn it that day in the basement. I run my fingers over the German words and then undo the clasp. Inside on the left is engraved the German word for *friendship*, *Freundschaft,* and on the right is a rather comical photo of a young woman, presumably Liesi. She's wearing a cook's white hat but a fake mustache covers much of her face! Out of curiosity, I remove the glass covering and then slip the picture out and turn it over. On the back is written *M. — Fasching Koch 1943*. M for Magdalena?

I pick up the telephone and dial Basti's number. When I hear his voice, I take my guess and run with it. "If Liesi's friendship locket had Magdalena's photo, did Magdalena have another with Liesi's photo?"

"Amazing, Ellen Troy. I wondered how long it would take you to figure that out. *Uroma* explained that the two of them began wearing those lockets when they started working together. Anyway, I thought you might find it intriguing."

"You're the best, Basti. It's a great gift and I have a feeling that somehow it's going to affect what we're doing."

When I hang up the phone, I put the locket around my neck and vow that I will wear it until this mystery is solved.

****

As spring drifts into summer however, the locket fades into the background of my life. Toward the end of June, I'm done with school but Basti's classes continue into July. I'm spending more time with Manon during the early summer vacation days and I'm happy when she invites me along on a day trip that she and her mom are making to Austria.

We leave early, traveling under a bluebird sky. As we head south toward the Alps, Mrs. Van Hoorn explains that she's visiting an old school friend who lives in Innsbrück. They plan to do a little shopping together and then have lunch somewhere.

"You girls are welcome to join us but, if you prefer, you may explore the city on your own."

We look at one another knowingly. It's a no-brainer; shopping and lunch with adults is bound to be boring.

Manon says, "Thanks, Mama. Ellen and I will explore."

Our first view of the city prompts Mrs. Van Hoorn to say, "See how Innsbrück straddles the Inn River, girls? That's how the city got its name. *Innsbrück* means *bridge over the Inn.*"

As we navigate through the narrow streets, I gaze at the steep mountains that run like a wall along the northern side and then at the series of mountains to the south that make up the impressive Tuxer range. "Yikes, this city is squeezed between some humongous Alps!"

"Yes, Ellen, but it's saved from remoteness by the two great highways that meet at a crossroads nearby. One can go east to Switzerland, north to Germany, or south to Italy at very high speeds."

In the city itself, the old town center is full of fancy old buildings that Mrs. Van Hoorn calls baroque style. As we head toward the eastern outskirts, things look more modern and we pull into her friend's driveway in a newer suburb at about ten.

Manon and I make the obligatory short visit to say hello and listen to Mrs. Van Hoorn's instructions on how to reach her in case of emergency. Promising to be back at the house by three, we hurry off to find adventure in the city.

Having been to Innsbrück before, Manon leads the way with confidence. We hop a tram heading toward the center and, a short time later, we're free and wandering through the *Altstadt* - the old city. We snack our way through the market, sniff flowers, and try on funky clothes at some of the stalls — all the while giggling and gossiping.

The weather is hot so we take a break sitting on the edge of a large fountain. We're dipping our toes into the water when Manon almost knocks me over with a question. "Sooo... is Basti your boyfriend?"

I feel the heat on my face rise and I avoid looking at her and stammer, "Basti? Why would you think that?"

"Well, for one thing, you blush when you talk about him."

"I do not!"

"Hah! You're blushing right now! Plus, I can tell he likes you too."

My skin feels prickly and I feel almost lightheaded but I manage to whisper, "How can you tell, Manon?"

"Well, let me count the ways — one, he spends a lot of time with you… two, the way he looks at you… three, he gave you a locket… "

"You don't understand, Manon."

"What I don't understand is why you deny liking a guy whose picture you're wearing close to your heart right now!"

"I… I do like Basti, Manon, but it's complicated."

Manon rolls her eyes and says, "You are complicated, Ellen. If a cute guy like Basti was that into me, I'd be shouting it from the nearest Alp!"

As we put our shoes back on and continue wandering, I feel a mix of emotions. I know that Basti spends a lot of time with me and he seems to like me but is it because I'm trying to help find Liesi or because he thinks I'm cute?... Hah! Who am I kidding? I'm not beautiful and I'm kind of geeky. I'm fifteen and have never had a boyfriend. Maybe boys don't see me that way — especially a hot boy

like Basti. I think he's totally cute but I can't tell him that —
can I? If I did, what would he say? What if he doesn't like me
that way? I might lose a friend. Am I trying to find Liesi to
make Basti like me or is it just me following the signs in my
dreams? It's all jumbled up in my mind because the dreams
are important to me but Basti is too.

Manon and I find ourselves on a street called *Innrain*
in front of an antique shop and we're drawn to the jumbled
display in the window.

"Oh look at that little porcelain mirror, Ellen. I would
love to have it for my bedroom but it probably costs a
fortune."

"It's nice, Manon, but all those flowers and cherubs
are too fancy for me. I like that tiny silver box with the bird on
top. I could use it for..."

*"Mein Gott, was für eines Medaillion und für eine
Amerikanerin!"*

The voice comes from an old man standing in the
doorway of the shop. The combination of not understanding
and the gruffness of his voice causes me to step back as he
approaches. Manon, however, steps in front of me and asks
him something in German.

His shoulders sag, he closes his eyes and seems to
meditate for a second. When he looks up, his eyes plead for
forgiveness and his voice softens and switches to English.

"I apologize if I have frightened you. I was so surprised… to see such a locket and on a girl speaking American English."

"Lots of American girls wear lockets," I say. "What's so surprising about mine?"

He actually blushes as he says, "It's because I have only ever seen two of these lockets in my entire lifetime and that was during the war."

Manon is practically hyperventilating when she asks, "Are you saying it's rare?"

"I can tell you for sure if I could take a closer look at it."

Turning to me, he says, "I would like to hear how you have come to possess it. Will you do me the honor of coming into my shop and letting me appraise it?"

I'm unsure. The thought of learning something about the locket's history is intriguing but I'm also a little weirded out that he wants us to go into the shop with him. I feel myself shaking as I say, "It's not for sale."

"Yes, of course. I promise only to have a look at it."

Okay, I have to trust my gut on this. He seems nice enough, there are two of us girls and this may be my only opportunity to find out more about this locket, so I agree. As Manon and I enter into the bowels of the shop she whispers, "Not only did Basti give you a locket, he gave you a rare antique! *That's* how much he likes you!"

I feel heat rise on my face despite the cooler air inside he shop.

In a messy cubicle that serves as his office, the shop owner removes boxes of gilded frames and yellowed music scores as he uncovers a spot for Manon and me to sit on a shabby sofa. Manon glances at me and I can see that she's feeling unsure about this. My own senses are on high alert too but I have to find out where this is going. I give Manon my most reassuring face and pray that I'm right. The shop owner walks over to his desk, rummages through the rubble in a drawer, and picks up a magnifying glass. He grabs the back of his chair, sits down backwards, and using his feet, wheels it toward us. With his hand reached out, he asks, "May I?" and I hand over the locket.

For several minutes, no sound is heard except for the ticking of a bunch of old clocks in the outer room. We watch as he eyeballs every detail on the locket's front and back before commenting. He notes the aged patina, the minor defects that signify use, the fine decorative touches, the clasp, the engraving, the sterling silver mark, and the mark that identifies the maker.

When he opens it to the fragile photo that is brittle with age, and the delicate script that identifies the young woman in the picture, Manon gasps, "It's not Basti!"

I whisper back, "I told you it's complicated, Manon."

The shopkeeper seems not to hear our exchange and, when he looks up, he is absolutely pale. His voice is a mere whisper of itself as the strangled word "Liesi" passes his lips. This time, my gasp is audible.

With a shocked voice, Manon says, "You know who this Liesi is, Ellen?"

I nod but, before I can say anything, we're both astonished to hear the shopkeeper begin to cry! We watch as he takes out a handkerchief, wipes his eyes, and then kisses the locket. Turning to us, he says, "I knew her," and then he begins to cry again.

I'm trembling with the thought of trying to explain things to Manon but I'm also bursting with questions to ask the shopkeeper. However, I force myself to wait until the man has composed himself and is ready to explain. When that moment comes, he is the one to ask the first question. "How have you come to wear this locket?"

"My friend, Basti, gave it to me for my birthday. It belonged to his great aunt Liesi."

When he is satisfied with my answer, he settles back into his chair and murmurs, "I expect that you want to know why seeing this locket has affected me so deeply."

I nod, and he says that, before he starts to tell us the story he needs to get some water. As we wait for him, Manon gushes, "It's a family heirloom? Basti is sooo… into you, Ellen."

Chapter 20 — *Herr* Fürstenrieder's Story

The shopkeeper returns with three bottles of water and hands one to each of us. Then he begins. "My name is Helmar Fürstenrieder and I was born in *München*. I'd known Liesi Falke since *Kindergärten*."

This seems to bring back a happy memory because he pauses and smiles in a dreamlike way.

"We were good students and went on to the same Gymnasium for high school. In those days we were almost inseparable. She was the first girl I kissed and I loved her. She said that she loved me too and I assumed that one day we would marry. We didn't discuss it; it just seemed that it would be a natural progression."

A tear rolls down the old man's cheek but the only thought I have is that I can't imagine happily ever after in high school!

"After we were both accepted into the university in 1939 — where she majored in medicine and I, in art history, we remained close for a while. However, as the war progressed and the Nazis interfered more with daily life, Liesi withdrew. When I asked her why, she said that she couldn't bear to think of love when hatred was engulfing our world."

"Excuse me, *Herr* Fürstenrieder but did you really expect Liesi to go on dates pretending that things were normal? The Nazis didn't just interfere, they terrorized!"

It's as if he doesn't hear me because he just continues his story.

"After university classes were suspended, I saw her even less. My few attempts to visit were greeted with apathy and she looked so listless that it worried me."

I notice that his hand is shaking as he reaches up to wipe his brow with a handkerchief, so I ask, "Are you okay, *Herr* Fürstenrieder?"

He takes a sip of water and says, "Yah, yah" and keeps going.

"Some months later, I ran into Liesi. She was with her friend, Magda. She looked like her old beautiful self but with a new vitality. When I remarked upon it, she said that she and Magda were working together at something purposeful. When I inquired about the nature of their work however, they were evasive, saying only that it was volunteer medical work. Then they changed the subject."

The pain on his face makes me feel for this man but I also wonder how Liesi felt. Was she just not into him any more or didn't she trust him? His next words capture my attention.

"I remember noticing that Liesi was wearing a locket and feeling a stab of jealousy. Curiosity got the better of me and I commented on its uniqueness. She told me that it wasn't unique because Magda had one as well. They were friendship lockets that had been given to them by a mutual friend."

My heart begins to speed up and I ask, "Do you know who the friend was, *Herr* Fürstenrieder?"

"No. She never said."

Disappointment washes over me but he's not finished.

"Desperate to know if she had a new boyfriend, I asked if it had a picture inside. She nodded and my heart ached but I braced myself and asked whom she had chosen. Her answer was surprising. The photos were of one another! They opened their clasps and showed me the amusing shots — a stab at humor during a stressful time."

"Did they actually say that the pictures were for fun?"

He doesn't answer my question, still lost in the past.

"I walked away from that encounter wishing that Liesi's playfulness had been shared with me. It was the last time I ever saw her."

His body seems to crumble at these last words and then he whispers, "I heard of their deaths in the bombing several weeks later."

"Bombing!?" Manon looks at me with wild eyes and I realize that I owe her an explanation, especially after she trusted my instinct to follow the crow in Samnaun.

I give her a quick hug and whisper, "I'll fill you in later, Manon. I promise." Then I focus on *Herr* Fürstenrieder and say, "After so many years, it's amazing that you recognized a locket you only saw once."

He sighs and says, "It's true that I saw *this* locket only once before but the other... that is a different story." He then reaches inside the crewneck of the lightweight sweater that he is wearing over a shirt and tie. Tugging on a thin silver chain, he withdraws a matching locket and my heart skips a beat. In silence, he undoes the clasp and Manon and I find ourselves staring at a woman with masked eyes and a powdered wig. Under her chin, she holds a sign that says *Mozart*. Then he removes the photo and shows the inscription *L - Fasching Wolfgang 1943!*

It's Liesi! My heart feels as if it will explode from adrenaline but I find myself unable to form words. Instead, I wait once again for him to explain.

"I came across this locket at an estate sale a couple of years ago. I thought it looked familiar and when I opened it and saw the remembered "Wolfie," photo I was overwhelmed. I had to bid on it. In the end, I was successful. I paid far more than its material value but to me, it is priceless."

He then looks at us, as if imploring us to understand and says, "I've never married you know. She was the only woman I ever loved."

How extraordinary! This man still carries the flame of love within his heart for a young, most likely dead woman who rejected him over 60 years ago. It's touching but also sad.

No one says anything for a minute or so and then, realizing that he's still holding the locket that I've given him, adds, "The reason that I was so moved by your locket is that I know it touched her skin. Mine has only her photo. I hope you will forgive my emotional outburst."

I nod my head but my mind is swirling. I surface when Manon nudges me. She had asked him if the estate sale was from Magdalena's family in *München*. Surprisingly, it wasn't.

I manage to ask, "Is it from *Herr* Johann König's estate in Samnaun, Switzerland by any chance?"

Manon's eyes almost bug out of her head as she mouths the words, "The cemetery?"

Herr Fürstenrieder's eyes also widen and he murmurs, "How very interesting. It was the estate of a König, but not Johann. The sale was from the effects of a Christoph König who had made a somewhat questionable name for himself as a nightclub owner in Innsbrück. He died at the age of sixty-two in what may have been a drug-deal-gone-wrong. The only person named in his will was his ex-wife Petra. She sold off his things in the estate sale and donated the profits to a local drug rehabilitation facility."

I'm stunned. I never thought to ask the priest in Samnaun if Johann König had any relatives and he didn't volunteer any more information. What was Christoph's relationship to Johann? My curiosity is piqued and I ask, "*Herr* Fürstenrieder, have you learned anything of the locket's history, other than what you already knew?"

"I had an opportunity to speak with the ex-wife and she knew only that Christoph's papa had sent it to him in 1994, the year before the old man died."

"That was a long time ago!"

"Yes it was, and it was before Petra knew him."

"Then how did she find out about it?"

"She said that Christoph wore the locket until he died. When he first showed it to her, she thought it was a curious gift, especially since it contained a photo of an unknown woman in a funny costume. When she said so, Christoph told her to mind her own business and refused to divulge the contents of the letter that accompanied it. She said it was indicative of the attitude that led to their divorce. Of course, the main reason was the drugs, but the attitude had cemented her decision."

"There was a *letter?*"

Herr Fürstenrieder nods and my skin feels prickly.

"Do you know where the letter is?"

"No. I'm sorry. It wasn't part of the estate sale that I remember."

My mind starts working overtime again. Liesi's locket was sent to Johann König's son! What was his connection to Liesi? I have to find that letter!

Herr Fürstenrieder changes the subject back to Liesi then and says, "I've often wondered since then if Liesi gave her locket to a man who captured her heart. As much as I loved her, I wouldn't have wished her unhappiness..." His voice trails off and he seems lost for a moment in another lifetime.

Feeling as if we have invaded a very personal space, I know that we should leave. Before we do though, I ask one last question, "Do you know the whereabouts of Christoph's ex-wife, *Herr* Fürstenrieder?"

He stands up and, as he hands the locket back to me says, "Petra still lives in Innsbrück, as far as I know. At the time of the estate sale, she was still using her married name. Since she and Christoph had a child together, I assume that she has kept it – unless, of course, she has remarried. I should have the old address in my records if you're interested."

I can barely control my excitement as I say, "Oh, I am!"

As we emerge from the darkness of the antique shop, we stop to allow our eyes to adjust to the sunlight. Manon looks me in the eye and says, "So... what was that all about?"

I tell her the short version of reading the diary and realizing that Liesi and Magda may have survived the bombing and fled using a network that the doctor they worked for had set up. I also tell her that, through Basti's *Uroma* Ana, we learned the name of the doctor. With the help of his family, we followed clues that led us to the network and Johann König,

"What I need to find out now, Manon, is what happened to Liesi and Magda after they reached Samnaun. Are they alive or dead? *Frau* Petra may help me find the answers."

I look at the scrap of paper in my hand. "Do you know how to get to this address?"

Manon checks her watch and says, "Yes, but we can't go there today. I didn't realize how late is it! We've got to get back or my mom will be upset."

I plead with her to call her mom to ask for more time. Manon dials the number of her mother's friend, but there's no answer. "They mustn't be back yet, Ellen. We really have to go. I'm sorry."

As we ride the bus back to the friend's house, I think about what has happened today. Can it be a coincidence? Or is it inevitable? I tend to believe the latter and I can't wait to tell Basti! He'll figure out a way to come back with me, of that I'm sure.

February 19, 1943

The news just kept getting worse. There was an arrest warrant out for Alex, and Willi was taken into custody at his apartment. Word is that Hans had the draft of a seventh letter in his pocket and the handwriting had been traced to Christoph, who had now also been arrested. There was only a small relief amongst the depressing events. She had managed to ask Magdalena if "Hansi" still had her "notebook." Feigning apology, Magdalena said that he had burned it with his trash. Her relief was such that a tear fell from her eye but she felt ashamed that Magdalena saw it.

February 23, 1943

As she walked away from the newsstand scanning the latest paper, the word Todesurteille jumped out at her from a short article. The death notice reported that the "people's" court had found Hans, Sophie and Christoph guilty the day before and they were EXECUTED by guillotine that very same day! This news slammed into her sensibility. None of them had reached their twenty-fifth birthday! Particularly sad was the tale of Christoph, whose wife had just given birth. He never even had a chance to meet his third child. She was beside herself with grief but at the same time afraid to express it. She hurried through the crowd toward the tram and home.

When she was alone, she walked over to the mirror in her room and studied her reflection. She didn't look chicken-hearted to the naked eye. But that's what she was — gutless, lily-livered, whatever you wanted to call it. Who was she kidding with her quest to become a healer, while millions around her were dying? How meaningless promising to "do no harm" would be, as if future lives saved would make up for the multitudes lost!

Chapter 21 — A Return

The dreams are getting more and more depressing and I'm starting to truly understand the terror that people felt under the Nazis. If someone who worked for a good cause during those evil times is reaching out for my help, it's important for me to solve the clues I'm being given. Once again, I record the dream in my diary and hope that a solution comes soon. Basti's family tree is also getting more and more mysterious — what is Liesi's connection to Johann and Christoph König?

Christoph and Sigrid Falke
great, great grandparents (built Haus Falke)

Dr. Anna (Falke) Schumann
great grandma (Uroma)

Elizabeth Falke
(Liesi) - (survived?)

(Gisela?)

(Johann König?)

Dr. Sabine Müller
grandma (Oma)

Christoph König(?)

Silke Hofstetter (m. Franz)
Parents

Sebastian (Basti) & Annika

Basti returns from class in the early afternoon and I ambush him before he turns into his front walk. He looks beat but he smiles when he sees me. "Hallo, Ellen Troy. Summer holiday seems to agree with you; you are positively glowing."

My words come gushing out in a torrent as I try to explain the important events of the day before. However, midway through, I can see that he isn't listening. "What's the matter, Basti? Don't you agree that we have to go and find her? Basti? Basti… what's wrong with you? Have you heard anything I said? And why are you staring at me?"

"What? I…I…I'm just glad you're here. I mean, looking so pretty and all and…" He seems uncomfortable all of a sudden. Shaking his head as if to clear the fog around it, he apologizes. Blaming it on intense lessons all morning, as well as hunger, thirst, and the heat, he begs me to give him time to shower, change, and eat. After that, he assures me, he will meet me at the fishpond and give me his full attention. Then he runs for his front door.

All thoughts of the new developments slip from my mind for a moment. He had said I was *pretty!*

****

Later at the fishpond, looking more relaxed and seeming more focused, he hears me out. He says that my story is *faszinierend.*

"Fascinating?"

"Yah, and I feel, not for the first time, that the things you learn are too incredible to be found by chance. It frightens me a little but it is also exciting. It makes me want to help you more."

"It's great to feel trusted, Basti. Thank you."

"So now what, Ellen Troy?"

"Well, tracing Magda's locket to the König family seems to confirm that at least one of the women was in Samnaun. Whether or not both of them made it or if one of them is in a grave marked Gisela von Werz is still to be determined. Since the only obvious path at the moment points to the ex-*Frau* Petra König, I think it's essential to speak with her."

"I agree."

"The problem is, as always, how do we get there, Basti?"

"Will Manon's mother be visiting her friend again soon?"

"No. I asked Manon but her mother usually visits only once or twice a year."

We mull over other options but we can't think of any way to convince our parents to take a trip before I leave Germany for Dad's next assignment in September. We don't have the excuse of ski season and we can't come up with any reasonable way to get permission to go alone. "Maybe it's time to get some adult help, Basti."

"There is someone I think we can trust to take us seriously, someone who might share our motivation to uncover the truth — my *Uroma*, Anna, Liesi's only sister. I...I told her a little bit about what you saw in the diary and asked her not to say anything to anyone else. I don't believe that she has and I suspect it sparked her interest. It may have had something to do with allowing me to give you Liesi's locket."

I smile and say, "Well, what are we waiting for then?" I'm up and striding off before Basti can answer. Together, we enter the yard at the rear of *Haus* Schumann. Nearer to the house, the lawn has a dappled look caused by sunspots that have filtered through the branches of a large chestnut tree. Further out, we can see his *Uroma* Anna in the full sunlight that bathes the garden. Her white hair is wrapped into a glistening thick braid that encircles her head. Bent over, hands reaching out to pluck her berries, a sunbeam brings to mind a coronation in a strawberry patch. Not wanting to startle her, Basti calls out before we approach. As her face turns toward us, we can almost feel the warmth of her smile.

She says that she is more than willing to listen but insists on her own list of priorities. First, we will have to help her wash and hull the berries. Second, she will pour us all some lemonade. Then we can settle into the comfy chairs in the shade of the chestnut tree where she will listen without distraction.

By the time we're ready to begin, she has added one more task. As impatient as we are, we don't object when she sets out a plate of homemade cookies.

It takes almost an hour for Basti to detail our findings in a mix of German and English, field *Uroma* Anna's questions, and make sure that we're both following along. My German has come along this year but it's still pretty basic and her English is rusty. Somehow we manage.

When Basti is finished, his *Uroma* whispers, *"Mein Gott!"* Then she says that she needs to think. I flush as I feel her eyes study me and evaluate my credibility. Then she clears her throat and begins speaking in rapid German to Basti. I find myself holding my breath. It's hard to read Basti's face as he listens and occasionally nods his head. After what seems like an eternity, he turns to me without expression and I anticipate bad news.

"*Uroma* Anna no longer drives but she thinks *Oma* Sabine might understand and be willing to take us."

"That sounds good but why aren't you smiling? Is something wrong, Basti?"

"*Uroma* has made one condition; we can only go to Innsbrück if we have our parents' permission."

"Is that a problem?"

"My parents might not react well to our secret trips. Even worse, your parents may be angry with me."

"'My parents will be fine when I tell them about the dreams and what we've learned so far. They're well aware of my unusual ability ever since Cuma and they won't blame you, Basti! Why are you worried about your parents if you were so confident that your *Uroma* would understand?"

First he just shrugs but then seeing the questioning in my eyes, he explains. "They were angry with me the day we got home late from Wolfratshausen and threatened to cancel my August trip to tennis camp in Italy. The only thing that saved me was that they believed me when I said we had been downtown with our friends all day. I got off with only a warning. If they now find out that I lied however, the camp will be history."

"Oh Basti."

I glance at *Uroma* Anna. She seems reasonable, at least from my own vantage point with limited understanding of German. Averting my eyes from the woman's scrutiny, I whisper to Basti, "She might not need to give your parents *every* little detail of our investigation so far, right?"

"*Nah jah,* I already tried that idea but *Uroma* is firm about the need for honesty. The one positive thing is that she is offering to back me up on the importance of what we have already accomplished. I just hope that my parents will appreciate it enough to forget my lie."

As we walk away from the session with his *Uroma*, I tell Basti, "Let's just hope for the best. If your parents don't freak out and your *Oma* Sabine agrees to drive us, there should be no problem."

His only response is "Hah!"

Seeing that he is so down, I change the subject. "Basti who do you think might have given the lockets to Liesi and Magda?"

"I'm guessing *Doktor* Grüber. Did you see their costumes? They could have been a code to remind them where to seek safe refuge."

This boy is good. "Of course! The 'Koch' and 'Wolfgang' were a clever way to remember *Herr* Koch in Wolfratshausen!"

Basti nods and then he adds, "I think their faces were covered in the photos because friendships among those who defied the Nazis were dangerous. If one of them were caught, a recognizable photo could betray the other. I'm surprised that they had written down even the first letters of their names, given the times."

Chapter 22 — Ex *Frau* König

What began as my intuition and a curious quest of two teenagers, mushrooms into a multi-family expedition. *Uroma* Anna suggests, perhaps wisely for Basti's sake, that my parents be present for her talk with Silke and Franz

Hofstetter. Though they're upset with their son, they choose not to make an issue of it in front of their American neighbors. Also, after hearing how important it seems to be to *Uroma* Anna, and how accepting of the extraordinary circumstances Mom and Dad seem to be, they agree that further exploration seems appropriate. Instead of allowing *Oma* Sabine to travel alone with Basti and me however, everyone expresses an interest in making the journey.

To add to the circus-like atmosphere, Manon spills the beans to her mother, and Mrs. Van Hoorn calls my mom with a helpful suggestion. She says that she has taken the liberty of contacting her friend in Innsbrück, who just happens to be on the board of the drug rehabilitation facility that received the donation from Petra König. If we would like, her friend, will be pleased to set up a meeting with the woman. She also says that they are both more than willing to come along to introduce us to *Frau* Petra.

****

So... on a warm Saturday in mid-July, a caravan of three cars holding eight adults and six kids (the whole van Hoorn family decided to join my family and Basti's family, including his *Oma* and *Uroma*!) winds its way south from Munich. We make our way snaking through the traffic jams of northern European holidaymakers bound for the sunny south.

Frau Petra König opens her door to us but she seems a bit hesitant. *Frau* Van Hoorn's friend, then takes over and in German, seems to do some explaining. She then makes the introductions. When she gets to me, she says more than just my name. I look at Basti and he translates, "This is Ellen Madigan, the one whose intuition started this investigation."

I ask Basti to tell *Frau* Petra that I couldn't have done it without his help and that we both have questions for her. Basti is reluctant to give himself credit so *Oma* Sabine translates my words.

Frau Petra then invites us all to sit down in her living room and directs her attention to Basti and me. In German, she says, "I don't think that I can help you very much because, though Christoph was the son of Johann König of Samnaun, Switzerland, he seldom spoke of his life there. I know only that he argued with his papa because he didn't want to go on to university and that he left home for good at the age of eighteen."

Basti asks, "So, Christoph ran to Innsbrück?"

"*Jah,* he came to Innsbrück and picked up odd jobs in the bars and pubs around the area called *Bögen.* It soon became obvious that he had a head for business and a natural talent for marketing the club scene. By the time that I met him, he owned two large discotheques and a café-bar."

All of this was said in German and I understood much of it but it's still hard for me to speak. I'm dying to ask some questions too so I tell her, *"Ich spreche nicht so gut Deutsch. Verstehen Sie Englisch, Frau König?"*

Luckily for me, she says that she does understand a little English and adds, *"Nah jah,* you speak English and I speak German, *gelt?"*

Okay. That's my cue to ask my first question. "How did you meet Christoph?"

She has a half-smile as she answers me and her German words become very soft. "I was out with friends and he flirted with me. I thought at first that he was too old. He was already 56 and I was only 31. However, he was very impressive. I was attracted to his confidence, his style, and his success. We had a whirlwind romance, married, and had a baby boy almost before I blinked."

Though the thought of such an old bridegroom is kind of freaky to me, I don't say it. Instead, I blurt out, "That is sooo romantic!"

Her reaction is unexpected. "Hah! The romance turned to disappointment. The clubs that were his success were also his downfall. That atmosphere attracts illegal activities and a lot of drug and alcohol abuse. In the end, his own growing drug habit made him unreliable. It was very sad."

Basti asks, "Is that why you weren't together?"

"Jah, I wanted a better environment for my son. I agreed to let Christoph visit him if he wasn't high but I

refused his financial support. It hasn't been easy but I've done it on my own and my son, Lukas, is turning into a fine young man. He is now twelve years old and an excellent student."

Basti nods and asks, "Will you tell us about Christoph's death?"

Frau Petra sighs and replies, " The drugs killed him. It was sudden but, for me, it had always been only a matter of time. It was very hard on my son. He was only six years old and he loved his papa, despite his faults."

Neither Basti nor I seem to be able to say anything right away. The silence is broken when *Frau* König adds, "I was surprised to be named in Christoph's will. I still didn't want his money so I had the estate sale and donated the profits."

That reminds me of *Herr* Fürstenrieder's locket so I ask her about it.

"Christoph told me only that it had come from his papa inside a letter. The only comment he ever made about it was, 'Too little too late.' When our son asked about the woman in the picture, he was told, 'No one I ever knew.' Christoph was wearing the locket when he died."

I'm practically holding my breath as I ask, "What happened to the letter, *Frau* Petra?"

"I looked for the letter but I didn't find it. I was hoping that it would explain things. Later on, Lukas told me why I didn't find it. He had been with Christoph when he came upon the letter among some papers one day. My son had watched in fascination as his papa re-read the letter and then threw it into the fireplace."

The meeting that began with optimism ends with our large group feeling somewhat deflated. Despite the disappointment, we vow to make the most of our long trek and enjoy our visit to Innsbrück. Though *Frau* Petra declines to join us, the rest of us enjoy a restaurant meal in the *Altstadt.* Afterwards, all three families thank *Frau* van Hoorn's friend for introducing us to *Frau* Petra, say goodbye to her, and then return to the guesthouse we checked into upon arrival.

****

At night, as I lay awake under the eiderdown comforter, I replay the day's story in my mind and one particular thing bothers me. Why would a man wear a locket from his papa that contained a picture of someone he hadn't known — especially someone whose face wasn't even recognizable and why would he burn the letter? I have a hard time falling asleep as my mind wrestles with that.

****

In the morning, as our families enjoy a breakfast buffet of juice, *Müsli,* fresh rolls served with butter, ham, cheese, honey, jam and Nutella, and sip on steaming cups of coffee and tea, I present my sticking point to Basti. He agrees that it's a dilemma but says that he feels we have perhaps reached the end of the line. Then seeing my sad face he adds, "If we're meant to finish this, Ellen Troy, I believe that the answer will find its way to you. In the meantime, I guess it's okay to just have fun today, isn't it?"

I smile at my friend and, despite my questioning mind, have to agree. In truth, I'm looking forward to visiting the highest zoo in the world, the mountainside *Alpenzoo*, and then taking the *Hungerburg* funicular ride. It will take us up to a high peak overlooking Innsbrück. With Basti, T.G., Manon and Marco all coming along, it will be a fun day. Basti's little sister Annika will be following us around as well, but she's okay for a kid. So, I decide to enjoy the day before it escapes.

****

During the long ride home, I use the time to update my diary once again. I still don't know Johann König's relationship to Liesi but I do know that he had a son, Christoph and now a grandson named Lukas.

Christoph and Sigrid Falke
great, great grandparents (built Haus Falke)

Dr. Anna (Falke) Schumann
great grandma (Uroma)

Elizabeth Falke
(Liesi) - (survived?)
(Gisela?)

(Johann König?)

Dr. Sabine Müller　　　　　　　*Christoph König*
Grandma (Oma)　　　　　　　　*(son-died 2008)*

Silke Hofstetter (m. Franz)　　*Lukas König (grandson)*
parents

Sebastian (Basti) & Annika

Chapter 23 — August

It's nearing the end of my year in *München*. I try not to focus on the unsolved mystery or on our family's impending departure at the beginning of September because I'm having a pretty great time. Basti is finished with classes and our group, which includes T.G., Marco and Manon, has grown closer since our trip to Innsbrück.

The five of us spend the first week of August hanging out and enjoying summer. We do everything and yet nothing together. We ride the bike paths, eat lunches and snacks on the grassy meadows of the city parks, tease one another over café tables, dive through the man-made waves at the *Wellenbad,* and lay around a lot listening to the *Deutsche Schlager* — the German hit parade songs that are the soundtrack of this summer.

The evening is warm and sticky and the forecast for tomorrow is hot. As our group sits dangling our feet into the Fish Fountain and spooning mouthfuls of lemon ice, Manon says, "It's so hot I wish I could be on the water. I've seen people rafting the Isar River and it looks fun."

That sounds good to me so I say, "Then let's do it!"

"The commercial trips are too expensive, Ellen."

T.G. becomes animated and says, "In the basement at home, I have an inflatable raft packed away! I'll have to check that it hasn't rotted in storage but, if it's okay, it can hold the five of us. What do you all think?"

Everyone thinks it's a cool idea (no pun intended) and before long we're all making a dash for the basement of *Haus* Falke.

****

In the morning, all five of us take the *S-Bahn* to Wolfratshausen and then walk to a riverbank put-in site lugging all of our gear. We use a hand pump to inflate the raft, strip down to our swimsuits, and stash our stuff on board. After pushing off, we're caught up in the gentle current and begin a lazy float back towards *München*

During the next several hours, we pass sleepy towns, wooded stands of trees, and grassy open areas. We encounter few people on the banks, except for the occasional sunbather stretched out on a towel or reading in a sand-chair.

From time to time, one of us jumps into the water and swims alongside. However, we're mostly just caught up in our own sunshiny world of giggles and stories and the joy of just chilling on the river as we float down it. Aside from devouring our packed lunches, it's pretty much a day of minimal exertion.

The only disruptions to this paradise are two things. The first occurs when we hear oompah band music. Manon squeals, jumps up and nearly falls into the river in the process. I grab her and say, "What on earth, Manon?"

"Look, Ellen! It's one of the commercial log floats I was telling you about. Oh, the people are waving to us! Wave back everyone!"

Basti isn't impressed and says, "*Na jah*, they're only waving because they are beer-drinking tourists."

T.G. says, "Hah! I'll wave in case they feel like throwing us some of that bratwurst they're grilling!"

"Yeah, the aroma is making me hungry," adds Marco.

My little brother and his friend are unbelievable. I ask, "How can you guys be hungry again? The two of you brought humongous lunches and I think you ate half of Manon's and mine as well!"

T.G. comes back with, "Hey, Basti helped too!"

Basti ignores this and shouts a warning instead. "Watch out and hold on!"

The words are barely out of his mouth when the big log float passes us at high speed and then moves off into the distance leaving a large wake for us to ride. After a few minutes of excitement and shouts of *"Yee haw!"* it's soon calm again.

The second disruption comes a little later when we come to a large dam in the river. Basti tells us, "We have to paddle to shore, carry the raft and go around it."

It's work but for only a short distance and we're soon on the river again. By the time the outline of the city comes into view, we're all feeling pretty mellow from the swaying of the raft and sunburned from the daylong exposure. It's with forced energy that we go ashore, deflate the raft and then trudge to the nearest tram for the ride home.

As the tram rocks and rolls, Basti tells me, "It's been a *fantastisch* day, Ellen Troy but you look tired. Lean your head on my shoulder if you need to."

Fantastisch doesn't even begin to describe it.

****

Easy, happy days continue for a time, until family plans prick our teenage bubble. All three families are leaving the city today, Saturday August 6th, for two-week vacations. The Van Hoorns are going to a holiday rental in Cyprus. Basti is heading to Italy — first to tennis camp for a week and then to join his family in Lake Garda. Our family is heading to southern France. We are going to pick up Cat in

Nice where she's been taking a summer French immersion course and then we will all drive to a small a rental apartment in the hill town of Seillan.

I've just finished helping to load the car when Basti appears. "So... you are about to leave, Ellen Troy?"

"Pretty soon, Basti. Hey, I hope tennis camp is fun."

"Thanks... It's been pretty fun here though."

His words wrap their warmth around me like a hug. "I've had fun too, Basti."

"*Na jah*, it's only two weeks and then we will have fun again, no?"

I feel my throat tighten as I say, "We can try but I won't have much time left here. My dad has pretty much finished preparing the museum exhibit. He says that we should be ready to move into the next phase of our lives about two weeks after returning to *München*."

Basti's face clouds, mirroring the depression I'm feeling. "But that's so soon! Where will you go?"

"I'm not sure yet, Basti. My dad's planning to use the vacation time to decide, with the help of the rest of us, between two very different career options for the coming year."

"I can't believe that you will leave yet, Ellen Troy. You haven't solved the mystery of Liesi and Magda and I believe that you are meant to do it."

"Well, I doubt there will be any clues in France but I promise I'll do my best to think of something."

Chapter 24 — Call for Help

As the rising spiral of the walled town of Seillans, France comes into view, T.G. yells, "Wow, It's built like a fortress! Any enemies attacking from the valley would be dead meat!"

He's right but I'm mesmerized by the way the ancient stones glow in the sun and I mutter, "Yeah, but it kind of looks warm and welcoming too. The way the sunlight is peaking through the spaces between the stones makes it look like the town is smiling, don't you think?"

T.G. crinkles his face. "I think the sun is affecting your brain, Ellen!"

As we head up the road, I ignore T.G. and cross my fingers that Seillans truly does welcome us and maybe gives me some ideas for how to solve the Liesi and Magda mystery.

Near the top of the town, Dad wedges the car into a tiny resident parking space and we climb out into the afternoon heat feeling wrinkled and sticky. At the edge of the parking area, we pass through an ancient archway and enter a narrow alley. We lug our bags over the cobblestones until we come to our apartment a short ways down on the right.

The place is tiny but Mom puts her positive spin on things. "Well, it seems that we are going to have a wonderful and authentic French experience!"

Despite living in a medieval fortress, we soon find that we are far from isolated. Seillans is crawling with vacationers and we hear all sorts of languages as we wander through town. Over the next few days we explore the surrounding areas. Soon each of us has a personal favorite place. Dad, of course, is partial to any of the Greek or Roman architectural remains and they seem to pop up everywhere. Cat was most excited with a day in Cannes ogling the mega-yachts, sitting at the stylish seaside cafes, and shopping the trendy boutiques. I have to admit that she rocks sunglasses. She seems to know it too — she has pairs to match every bikini color and she has a *lot* of bikinis! T.G.'s favorite was a trip inland to "the grand Canyon of France," the *Gorges du Verdun*. He's still trying to figure out how a small chapel was built on top of one of the steep-sided peaks we passed along the way. Mom loves the markets and each town seems to have a special market day. She says that she loves the scents of lavender and spices and she can't get over the innumerable versions of goat cheese. The artist in her also loves the brilliant colors of the textiles, fresh fruits and vegetables, and the canvases of local painters. For me, the highlight was taking a ferry to the Iles de Lerins, the park-like islands just offshore from Cannes. I had a blast exploring the wooded paths and swimming and picnicking along the rocky shore.

None of us are bored, that's for sure. In fact, our days are so full that I barely think about Christoph König's locket or the whereabouts of Elisabeth (Liesi) Falke and Magdalena (Magda) Alt. I do think of my friends though... Basti enjoying tennis camp... Manon and Marco having fun in Cyprus.

It's midway through the second week and I'm sitting on the steps by the courtyard wondering if they think of me at all or if they're too busy with newfound friends. They have probably struck up conversations with lots of new kids — unlike French-language-deficient me. I'm having an okay time with my family — no... better than okay, but I miss my friends. After vacation we will have so little time before I have to leave *München* and it makes me sad. I just wish that I could at least talk to them. I wonder why I'm feeling this way. It's as if my antenna is sparking and senses the need to communicate.

My self-pity is interrupted by Mom 's voice calling me from the balcony. "Mrs. Van Hoorn has just called from Cyprus and she wants to speak with *you*, Ellen!"

I run up the steps and around to the front door. My heart is pounding as I rush inside and skid to a stop. Then *Frau* van Hoorn's words stun me.

"Ellen, I'm sorry to interrupt your family holiday but Petra König called me in a panic and insisted that you were the only one who might help. Personally, I wasn't sure it was the right thing to do, but Manon convinced me."

I feel as if an electric jolt has just run through me. I was right; someone *had* been trying to communicate! I'm trembling but I manage to say, "I'll help if I can, Frau van Hoorn. What's the problem?"

"Petra received a phone call from a doctor named MacDougal in California who spoke German and said she needed to speak with Christoph König."

"But Christoph is dead!"

"Exactly, Ellen, but the doctor's reaction after Petra told her that, is why Petra called me."

"What happened?"

" She said that Doctor MacDougal began to cry and say that she was dying. Then she apologized for being too late to tell him about his mother."

"Christoph's mother had a secret? I hope Frau Petra asked what it was!"

"She was about to when Doctor MacDougal sobbed and said, 'I'm so sorry… so sorry' and then hung up the phone!"

"Did *Frau* Petra call her back?"

"Yes, Ellen. She said that she tried several times. However, there was no answer, just a voice message in English that she didn't understand. Now Petra is frantic because the phone call is making her imagination run wild and she wonders if it is somehow connected to the locket that Christoph wouldn't talk about. Though it no longer matters for him, she worries how a family secret might affect her son."

"Someone has to find Doctor MacDougal!"

"Petra asked if you would be willing to try, Ellen."

My head is spinning but I assure Frau van Hoorn that I'll give it my best shot.

After I hang up, Mom is waiting and curious, so I give her a quick recap.

"She wants you to find this woman in America? What is she thinking? You're fifteen years old!"

"I may be only fifteen years old but I can make a phone call."

"You are not handling this yourself, Ellen. There will have to be another way."

I'm itching to act on this because all my senses are telling me this is important. I push myself to think hard until a plan comes to mind.

"I have another idea but first I need to find Basti in Italy and phone him."

"I know that your ideas are sometimes great, Ellen, but this one will have to wait. You are *not* calling Basti now. This is family time... for both of you. Besides, you'll see him in a few days."

"But, Mom..."

"There's no 'but', Ellen. Family time, remember?"

There is no point in asking to return to *München* a couple of days early either. First of all, I know it won't fly and second, what I need to do once I get there requires Basti's help and he won't return until Saturday either. So, temporarily unable to do anything about it but think, I spend my quiet moments planning a course of action and hoping that the woman in California doesn't die before I can find her.

****

Quiet moments are hard to come by though. We pack in as much activity as we can and try to accommodate everyone's interests. We beach, hike, hang out, and most of all, laugh.

This morning, I grab my jeans and a tee and slip into them. I'm about to leave the room when Cat's voice stops me in my tracks.

"You've got to be kidding me!"

I turn around to see my sister sitting upright in bed looking groggy but still fashionable in black and white polka-dotted pjs and a pink satin sleep mask pulled up on her cream-skinned forehead. She looks like a magazine ad. However, ads don't ask questions so I answer her.

"I didn't even say anything. How could I kid you?"

"Oh Ellen, just look at those jeans!"

I glance down looking for stains, but don't see any.

"What's wrong with them?"

Cat throws back her covers, springs out of bed and comes at me with determination. Then she grabs a fistful of my baggy jeans and says, "Are you planning to invite a friend to hop in there with you today?"

"Let go and leave me alone, Cat!"

"Why? So you can continue to dress like a sloppy boy?"

"I'm comfortable… and you're just mean!"

"I'm not trying to be mean. I'm just trying to help… You know, you have a nice shape. I think a sleeker look would show that off."

"Well I don't have any so-called sleek clothes so you might as well forget about it."

"Look, Ellen. Why don't you try on a pair of *my* jeans? If you like the look, maybe we can convince Mom and Dad to let you get some new ones that fit better."

To get her off my case, I agree to try them on and also try a more fitted shirt. Go figure. It's kind of a miracle. Cat may be way too into this stuff for my taste but she *is* good.

I have to admit that I'll miss her. Since it's already been decided that four of us will be leaving Europe soon and Cat is staying at university in France, I won't see her again until Christmas when she visits us.

****

When Saturday morning arrives, I feel teary as I hug Cat before she boards her flight to Paris.

Her final words to me are, "You look great, Ellen. I'm glad Mom let you get some clothes that fit better. Boys will notice for sure."

I wave good-bye and then join the rest of my family for the long trek home to *München*. It will give me lots of time to think about Doctor MacDougal and what I need to do.

August 1943

Despair continued to wash over Liesi and it only deepened as she learned in later months of other heroes in her sorry midst, including Professor Huber who had gone to the guillotine with Alex. To add to the distress, Allied bombing of the city was a constant threat. The nerve-wracking air raid sirens frayed her nerves and the long nights of terror in the shelter left her tired and overwrought. Lectures at the Universität had been suspended and she retreated into self-loathing and fear. It was Magdalena who saved her from total despair.

It was late morning when the doorbell rang, and she opened it to find Magdalena pacing back and forth. "Ah, finally! I was beginning to think you left."

The pacing stopped and she could see by the reaction on Magdalena's face that she must look a fright. She heard the hiss of her words, "My God, you look pale!" After a moment's hesitation, Magdalena's voice took on a more confident and upbeat tone, "But I have just the solution on this beautiful summer day — a trip to the countryside!"

The sunlight hurt Liesi's eyes and Magdalena's sudden appearance and cheery disposition was overwhelming. "Are you mad? I couldn't." She started to back away and close the door but Magdalena would have none of it.

Magdalena placed her foot in the doorway and urgency seemed to take hold of her. "You don't understand! I need you to come to the countryside. WE need you to come. And, whether you realize it or not, YOU need you to come!"

Fear and shame had almost robbed Liesi of the ability to react but she managed to squeak out, "What I need is for this damned war to be over."

Just then, a small voice called out. "Magda! Komm mal!"

She turned in the direction of the voice and, for the first time, noticed an automobile parked in front of her house. To her amazement, there were children in the back seat!

Magdalena turned and called out, "Ich komme schon!" and then she turned back to her friend and berated her. "You want this war to be over? And then what, will the only Germans left be morally bankrupt? We can't let that happen, don't you see? If we do nothing, Hitler will have sucked all the pride and hope out of what's left of the German people!"

Liesi's face was blank as she asked, "And going to the countryside will restore pride and hope?"

"Yes, and I'll tell you why. Since 1940, the regime has been evacuating children, and even whole school classes, from the cities by train to escape the bombing. The fairytale

is that they will have a holiday in the farmland enjoying sunshine and safety – the so-called Kinderlandverschickung. What they fail to mention is that their Nazi education will be continued without any input from parents or non-party influences. In effect, they are creating select environments for grooming the next generation to hate."

When Magdalena finished, Liesi nodded toward the vehicle and asked, "And you're bringing more children to be indoctrinated as Nazis?"

"No. That's the beauty of it. I'm bringing these children to private homes in the clean country air — homes that a Doktor requests for children too ill to attend regular school. The Doktor knows that these families are committed to home-schooling children with respect for human life and without propaganda. These homes have real heroes who will teach these youngsters the truth."

"But Magdalena, how can you be sure? How do you know that it's not a trap and that you won't end up being arrested?"

"Truthfully? I don't know. But at some point, each of us has to make a choice. Do we become part of the problem through inaction or do we work for change? What I am doing is something very small but at least it is something I'll be able to live with."

Liesi was still unconvinced. "Magdalena, you're driving a car! Isn't that asking to be caught? And besides, how did you get the petrol... or the permit for that matter?"

"Since the air raids began, I've been working for Doktor Grüber. It's his car and as a physician he is allowed to have one to help care for air raid victims. He does help them but his main concern is the children and these private homes help his patients. He is a good man and I trust him."

"Are these children sick then?"

"Hah! They have a malignancy of spirit that must be rooted out. But that's not what is written on their records." She sighed and then murmured, "So... I really could use some help. Will you do it then?"

Liesi was about to refuse when she caught sight of a young boy who looked to be about ten emerging from the car and heading toward them. He was dressed in the shorts and shirt of the Deutsches Jungvolk — the younger version of the Hitler Youth. Something about that image settled it for her. "I'll do it... if only to make sure that child and others like him will never have to wear that uniform again."

Chapter 25 — Transatlantic Call

By the time our car pulls up in front of *Haus* Falke, it's already 2 a.m. Sunday morning. I slept for most of the car ride and I had another dream — an important one! At last, it confirmed that the dreams *are* about Liesi! It also filled in the missing details of the stories we've heard. I now know for sure that uncovering Liesi and Magdalena's fate is truly the mission this place has given me. I'm more motivated than ever to bring it to a conclusion because the dreams have emphasized to me how much fear Liesi had to overcome and how courageous very small groups of people were in the midst of rampant evil. Whatever the outcome proves to be, I want Basti to have these facts before I leave Germany. It will be one small thing I can do for a friend who has believed in me.

My heart leaps when I see that the Hofstetter's car has already returned. It's the middle of the night though so I will have to wait until morning to see Basti.

****

I have a hard time sleeping so I'm up early. I record the dream I had in the car before I forget the details. When I finish with the diary, I make a copy of all seven dreams for Basti.

As I head for the door after breakfast however, Dad reminds me that I need to help unload the car. It's a pain but

I do as I'm told. Then I take off like a flash and head for next door.

Before I can touch the doorbell, the entrance flies open and I'm dumbstruck. Basti looks different. His skin is bronzed, his hair is sun-bleached, and he looks even cuter than before! It's not until he smiles that I realize he's the same.

Before I find myself able to speak again, he says, "France agrees with you... you look nice ... I mean you always look nice but... "

Inside I'm shouting, *thank you, Cat!* I try not to blush and just say, "Thanks, Basti, but I'm just wearing new jeans." Then I change the subject and waste no time telling him about the woman in America.

"Let me guess. You want to find her, don't you, Ellen Troy?"

"I do and I have an idea."

"Well then, you'd better come in and explain our plan over breakfast."

As I follow him to the kitchen, I smile to myself; he said, "*our* plan"! I take this as my cue to give him my packet of dreams. I sip some tea as he reads them and chews his breakfast. I watch his face for a reaction and I can see that he is moved. When he finishes, he looks into my eyes and whispers, "You're amazing."

I feel the heat rise on my face and I can barely think straight. Then I give myself a mental slap and stand up. "We need to make a phone call, Basti. I'll explain as we walk to the phone booth."

If Basti thinks I'm acting weird, he says nothing. He just follows me out the door. When he catches up, I explain my plan.

At the booth by Rewe, he makes the phone call that I suggested and we soon have an appointment for the afternoon with *Doktor* Erika Grüber. He says, "She was surprised to hear from us again and amazed to learn that, although her uncle's two young assistants missed their rendezvous with him, they were able to escape. She is also intrigued that a dying physician in California seems to have a connection to them."

Basti's next words electrify me. "*Doktor* Erika told me something else; *Doktor* Heribert Grüber had a child! A son! He lives in San Francisco."

****

When we arrive at her office a few hours later, *Doktor* Erika greets us like old friends. She's full of questions and it's obvious that her mind has been speculating about both the women and her uncle. "Is it possible that Liesi and Magda went to California too? Did *Onkle* Heribert know this? Could he have even been involved? If so, why wouldn't he have mentioned it, especially since the war was long over? Why wouldn't their families have been informed?"

We have no immediate answers to her rapid-fire questions but lucky for us, she is determined to help us find them. We tell her what we do know — that they might have made it to Switzerland. Then we try to give her a satisfactory understanding of the situation.

"Will you contact *Doktor* Heribert's son for us, *Doktor* Erika?"

"Yes. I think that is a good idea, Ellen." She looks at her watch then and says, "Well, it is now about half past 2. That means it is about 8 in the morning in America…"

I interrupt. "That's on the east coast. It's only 5 am in California."

"Na jah… Cousin Martin is a very early riser."

She places the call and, from what we can surmise hearing only one end of the conversation, Cousin Martin isn't that early of a riser. We listen as *Doktor* Erika assures him that no one has died, there is no emergency, and that she is truly sorry for alarming him with such an early call.

When all that is out of the way, it becomes harder for me to follow along. Though she is speaking in English to her American cousin, I can't hear what he is saying on the other end. The call seems interminable but when it ends, *Doktor* Erika has a lot to tell us. "I think that I have just sent shockwaves through my cousin. He said that his papa was haunted by that night of escape so long ago and yearned to know the fate of the two young women who never arrived at the meeting place. Despite their fear, both women had shown tremendous courage and had earned his respect and trust. He feared that they had both been injured or died in the bombing or had been killed or imprisoned by the Nazis and he blamed himself for putting them in harm's way. Martin said that *Oncle* Heribert would have been at peace when he died if he knew that they had made it to safety."

I'm excited that we really do have a California connection and I have to ask the critical question. "*Doktor* Erika, is your cousin, Martin, willing to help us find this woman, Doctor MacDougal?"

"Yes, Ellen. The name MacDougal means nothing to him but he is intrigued that she appears to have some connection to Samnaun. It's where the women were heading and *Oncle* Heribert also had a short stay there with Johann König. If she knows anything about the fate of either Liesi or Magda, he says he would like to help us find out because it would have been important to his father."

"Great! Does he have a plan?"

"Ah, Ellen, we have just surprised him with this! You must give him time."

"But time is running out — for me anyway. I'll be leaving Germany soon and I can't finish this if I'm not here!"

"Stay calm. Martin promised to get back to me as quickly as possible. He'll call the number and, if that doesn't work, he'll search online for an address to go with that number. It won't work if she called from a cell phone though. In that case, he has another idea. Like his papa, he is also a medical doctor and has connections in the medical community. He does not know of a Doctor MacDougal in the San Francisco Bay area where he lives but realizes that she could be anywhere in the state. He will try to find her but, since it is a Sunday, he may not have much information until tomorrow when the workweek resumes."

"Bummer."

Doktor Erika says, "You must trust that he will do his best. I will call you as soon as I hear anything."

We have no other choice so Basti and I stand up, shake her hand, and thank her for her help. Then we say goodbye.

The elevator door is just about to close when we hear, *"Moment mal!"* and see her running toward us. Basti leans his shoulder between the doors to stop them from closing and then grabs my hand and pulls me through with him. We stumble to a halt, just inches from the spot where *Doktor* Erika stands catching her breath. "He called right back! He… he had a California Medical Association directory online and was able to look up MacDougal. He also said that he's going to Santa Barbara right away and will keep me posted."

"Doctor MacDougal's in Santa Barbara?" I ask.

"I'm not sure. He didn't explain much. He just said that he had already called a taxi to take him to the airport. It will be a bit of a trek because he could only get a flight to Los Angeles so he will rent a car and drive to Santa Barbara."

Basti and I say goodbye again and hope that Doctor Martin's trek will be worth it.

Chapter 26 — Waiting for Doctor Martin

I'm tense. Basti and I spoke with *Doktor* Erika Grüber on Sunday but now it's Wednesday and we still haven't heard anything. The worst part is that my time in Germany is running out. Mom has started packing things up and we leave in 9 days! How can I just leave when Basti needs my help? We have to finish unraveling his family mystery!

To compound the pressure, Dad has proposed taking us to the middle of nowhere for next year and Mom and T.G. agree! How can I be happy there when I've voted against it? I've never been against a move before. It's a definite first for me and it's somewhat disturbing. Am I starting to let my feelings for Basti affect my sense of adventure?

****

Finally on Friday, Basti sprints into our garden where he finds me by the pond and announces, "*Doktor* Erika called me, Ellen Troy."

He probably expects me to greet the news with excitement but the eyes that look up at him reveal no excitement, only tears.

His face clouds over and he mumbles, "If it's a bad time I can come back later."

"Please stay."

His reaction is hard to read. Is he happy not to be banished or is he worried about having to listen to something too personal? He says nothing as he takes a seat beside me.

I continue to sniffle and dab at my eyes while Basti waits. He seems uncomfortable and probably hopes that I will smile and say, "Only kidding!" I know that I have to get myself together so I purse my lips, blow out an audible cleansing breath, and look up. My tear-streaked face struggles not to betray any more emotion. "Sorry about that... I seem to be having trouble leaving here. It's very uncharacteristic." I switch my voice to a perkier tone and say, "So... let's start again. Hi, Basti! Any news?"

For a moment, he just stares at me with a funny look on his face but then he says, "Is there any special reason you don't want to leave, Ellen Troy?"

Not wanting to say anything silly and humiliate myself, I just say, "I guess I'll just miss my friends."

His eyes search my face and I think I might die of embarrassment. I force my eyes to avoid his and ask again, "So, any news, Basti?"

When I still get no reaction, I snap my fingers in front of his eyes and yell, "ANY NEWS, BASTI?"

Startled back into the moment, he shakes his head as if to clear the cobwebs and mutters, "Nah jah, it's just a lot to think about... *Doktor* Erika... she gave me the bad news first; Doctor MacDougal is dead."

"No!"

"Yah, I felt like my heart would stop when I heard those words. Then it started beating faster when she said that her cousin had spoken with Doctor MacDougal before she passed and that he learned the fate of Liesi and Magda!"

"And?"

"I was holding my breath as I waited for the details but *Doktor* Erika didn't give me any. She said that her cousin would reveal nothing more by phone."

"Are you kidding me?"

"No, but guess what? Doctor Martin is coming to *München*! He wants to deal with things in person. So we will all have to wait until after his arrival next Tuesday."

My embarrassment and also my sadness are soon forgotten because Tuesday is only 4 days before I leave Germany! I swing into plan mode and rattle off a list of "to-dos" to Basti:

"One, we need to meet with *Doktor* Erika's cousin, Martin, as soon as he arrives.

Two, your *Uroma* Anna will need to be informed of her sister's fate, whatever it was.

Three, *Frau* Petra needs to be told any information that is related to her son.

Four, anything else that needs to be done will depend on what Doctor Martin has learned."

When I finish, I wait for a reaction but there is none. "Geez, Basti, get with it! Have I forgotten anything?"

He just smiles first and then says, "It's perfect. I will make sure our meeting happens as soon as possible. Doctor Martin Grüber will be delighted to meet you, I'm sure."

Just before he exits the garden, he hesitates and turns to face me. "I hope I am one of the friends you will miss, Ellen Troy."

He's gone before I can reply but I find myself crying again and this time I'm both happy and sad.

****

Doctor Martin Grüber's flight touches down onto German soil on a Tuesday morning of blue skies dotted with cotton ball clouds — the colors of his papa's Bavarian flag. Unlike most natives though, Doctor Martin probably enjoys the weather. Locals, on the other hand, complain that the breeze moving the picture-perfect weather over the Alps often descends on *München* and increases the atmospheric pressure, which cause headaches and other physical aliments. They call it the *Föhn.* I've lived here for a year and it has never bothered me. I mean, I get cramps sometimes but I blame those on hormones, not the alpine weather!

We hear nothing until the next day. Basti and I are hanging out by his house phone when *Doktor* Erika calls. Basti picks up and she tells him, "I met my cousin at the airport and we had a happy reunion with my parents, then a light lunch. Then Martin excused himself and settled in for a nap. I think the stress of this trip on top of the Santa Barbara one, plus the heaviness in his heart, seems to have wearied him because he didn't wake up until this morning! He really is anxious to meet you both but I want to give him a little more time to adjust. Would the two of you and your *Uroma* Anna like to come over to my apartment tomorrow morning to meet him?"

We're forced to endure another day of agonizing anticipation but of course we say that we will be there.

Doktor Erika also asks Basti to contact *Frau* Petra about setting up a meeting with Doctor Martin and to call her back. *Frau* Petra agrees to meet with Doctor Martin in Innsbrück on Friday, the day after our own scheduled meeting. Basti relays the message and it's all set.

At home, I tell Mom and Dad about tomorrow's meeting and Mom says, "That's great, Ellen! You'll have all your answers with time to spare before we leave the country."

"Maybe, but *Frau* König can't meet with Doctor Martin until Friday. What if there's more to learn and I'm not there?"

Always the optimist, Mom says, "If there 's anything important, I'm sure Doctor Martin will fill you in."

I hope so. Friday is calling it close for me. It's the day before we leave and I'm getting more stressed by the minute.

Chapter 27 — Coming Together

I've barely been able to sleep. It's Thursday morning and I'm at the Hofstetter's door well before the expected hour. However, Basti and his *Uroma* Anna are already dressed and waiting. They haven't slept much either.

None of us talk much on the tram ride over and it's with a mixture of excitement and unease that we enter *Doktor* Erika Grüber's home. It's a warm September day and she leads us outside to a small-enclosed garden where her cousin Martin sits under the shade of a vine-covered pergola.

Martin is a healthy-looking older guy wearing a knit polo and khakis, fitting my vision of California casual. He stands as we enter and makes his way over to *Uroma* Anna. He takes both of her hands in his, as if to steady her for what he has to say. "Ah, *Frau Doktor* Schumann, *danke schön…*

for coming…" He stops after that and seems at a loss for words. Seeing her cousin's unease, *Doktor* Erika gently interrupts. She guides *Uroma* Anna to a seat and then introduces Basti and me. "Martin, these are the two clever young people I've been telling you about, Ellen Madigan and Sebastian Hofstetter."

To us she says, "May I present my cousin, Doctor Martin Grüber."

His face brightens as he smiles and shakes hands with us. "Call me Martin," he says. Then he looks at me. "I understand that your insight and persistence has led to all of this. Very cool." He then turns to Basti. "And you have found a friend with a key to your family history. You've been smart to follow her lead. Good instinct." Addressing both of us, he adds, "I am ever so grateful to you both. Because of you, I have learned much about my father, his wartime associates and their incredibly long journeys." Then he smiles and explains, "I mean that literally — they actually *walked* to their new lives!"

"You look like you walk a lot yourself, Doctor Martin."

"Oh I do, Ellen. The hills of San Francisco help to keep me in shape." His voice gets quiet. "They are challenging but they pale in comparison to the mountains my father and the others climbed."

Not knowing how to respond, I just nod.

Doktor Erika suggests that we all take seats and then she pours us each some iced tea and we settle in to listen to his story.

Doctor Martin apologizes for his poor German ability but says that he will try. However, *Uroma* Anna tells him to speak English. If there is something she doesn't understand, she will ask Basti to translate.

"As I drove north toward Santa Barbara from the L.A. airport, I headed for the only address I had been able to find — her pediatric office. I prayed that someone would be there who could help me reach the dying woman before it was too late.

"At the office, I was relieved to find that Doctor Ute MacDougal was listed in partnership with two other physicians. As a professional courtesy, one of her colleagues agreed to see me. Afterwards, he was kind enough to make a phone call to her home on my behalf and her husband, John, spoke with me."

Why am I disappointed that her name is Ute? Deep down, was I really expecting it to be Liesi or Magda?

"John warned me that Ute's condition was grave and that she was often sedated to ease the pain. However, when I told him of the Samnaun connection and that my father might be an old friend of hers from the war, he agreed to a visit. He said that he would ask the nurse to ease up on the medication for a short period so that Ute might be lucid when

I arrived. He did caution me that if it became too painful for his wife, the visit would be terminated. This brought a new sense of urgency and I sped toward their home in the foothills of the Santa Ynez Mountains."

I glance over at Basti and his *Uroma* and see the intensity on their faces, as if they are willing Ute MacDougal to wait for Doctor Martin's arrival.

"John MacDougal was waiting for me at the front door. Before he made a move toward his wife's room, he said what was on his mind. 'Doctor Grüber, you said on the phone that this was related to my wife's phone call to Austria. I know that it was important to her but I thought that the matter had been resolved. I would hate to see her needlessly upset.'

"I felt empathy for this man because I could almost feel how much he cared. I cared too and I spoke from my heart. 'Mr. MacDougal, for almost forty years my father grieved for two lost friends. I now have reason to believe that your wife may be able to shed light on their fate, as well as on the fate of a child in Innsbrück. It would make both my family and a young boy very grateful to have some closure. I beg your forgiveness for this intrusion and ask for your help.'"

My mouth is dry and my heart is thumping. I want to shout that we all need closure but I force myself to be patient.

"John MacDougal nodded and then led me forward. As I entered the room, the eyes of the wasted figure in the bed met mine with what seemed like recognition and I felt confused. Before I could say anything, she managed to speak first, not to me but to her husband. *'Liebling,* I would like you to meet the man who saved my life during the war.' I suddenly remembered how much I looked like my father."

I'm confused. Why would she think Doctor Martin was his father? Did the medication make her thinking fuzzy? And could she really be…? My thoughts are interrupted when I realize that Doctor Martin has stopped speaking. His eyes are closed and he seems emotional.

Concern shows on *Doktor* Erika's face but she's careful not to embarrass her cousin. Instead, she suggests, "Why don't we all take a break and have something to eat before my cousin continues? I purchased a lovely teacake just this morning and I, for one, am quite hungry."

None of us are really hungry but we eat in silence and hope that Doctor Martin will be able to continue when we're done.

Chapter 28 — Reunion

Doctor Martin excuses himself and goes inside. When he returns to the garden, he seems in control of his emotions once again. He apologizes for the delay and says that he is ready to continue, if we are.

Is he kidding? Of course we are.

"Doctor MacDougal had mistaken me for my father and, although she was 40 years older than when she knew my papa and physically ravaged by cancer, I had a feeling that my father would have recognized this woman. I was at a loss though — Doctor MacDougal had to be Liesi or Magda, but which one?"

There are several shocked gasps, mine possibly being the loudest.

"I was about to explain who I was and ask her true identity when she cut me off. The dying doctor looked at me, eyes begging for agreement, and posed a pointed question. 'You *do* remember your little helper, Ute Seidl, don't you, *Herr Doktor* Grüber?'"

Ute Seidl? I'm getting so confused that my head is swirling.

"I didn't understand the reason for the deception, but I nodded just the same and said, 'You were a true heroine, Ute, and Heribert Grüber is thankful to know that you've been safe all these many years.' It was stretching the truth but I hoped in my heart that my father's spirit was watching this. Also, I didn't have the heart to tell her that he was dead and be the cause of more pain.

"She smiled then and turned to her husband, John. She said that it would please her to have a few moments alone with her old friend. Would he mind? There was so much to catch up on... *and so little time*. She didn't say the last part out loud, but it was understood by all of us. John agreed to her request and seemed okay with the fact that she mistook me for my father. He just cautioned her to not overdo it and said he would give us fifteen minutes. He kissed her cheek, cast a pleading glance at me to take care of her, and then he left us alone."

My brain is screaming, *tell us which one she really is!*

"When I asked her why she never told John her real name, she sighed and said, 'When the war ended, I wanted to leave Switzerland and return to *München* but it was a terrible time...' The words seemed to take a lot out of her and I sensed that she was in pain. I offered to call for John but she was adamant and said, 'No, not yet. There's something else... another story...' She was in distress then, and I knew that I had to summon help. I got up to leave but she grabbed my coat sleeve and whispered, 'John knows the story except for the real name... Gisela was Liesi...'"

There is another audible chorus of gasps and *Uroma* Anna moans. Gisela von Werz, who is buried in Samnaun, really is Elizabeth (Liesi) Falke! I lock eyes with Basti and, with tears in his eyes, he whispers, "You found her, Ellen Troy. You truly did."

I whisper back. "*We* found her, Basti. No, *we* found them *both*. Ute is Magda, for sure."

Basti shivers and then hugs *Uroma* Anna. She draws me into their embrace too.

Doctor Martin gives us all a moment and then he continues. "Ute's grip loosened on my sleeve and I whispered, 'Thank you Magda.' She nodded and I ran to get John."

Yes! Ute Seidl MacDougal really was Magdalena Alt!

"She lived for two more days in a mercifully medicated haze. John MacDougal allowed me to sit by his side and I grieved with him and his family. It gave John some comfort to hear of 'Ute Seidl's' intrepid exploits during the war and he looked at his sleeping partner with renewed admiration and pride. In turn, he revealed his wife's main regret and the story of 'Gisela' as he knew it."

At this point, *Uroma* Anna is weeping and Doctor Martin seems exhausted. Realizing that it may be too much for them all at once, *Doktor* Erika suggests that we stop for the day. Basti and I are speechless. We want to hear the story of "Gisela"/Liesi and we're running out of time — well, *I'm* running out of time!

Doktor Erika notices our startled expressions and says, "Of course you must hear the rest of the story. Cousin Martin also needs to tell it to *Frau* Petra König so, if you don't mind coming along to Innsbrück tomorrow morning, he will only have to tell it once. What do you think?"

Basti and I both blurt out, "Yes!" We look at *Uroma* Anna then and, to our great relief, she nods. For me, it's down to the wire and I don't want to miss my last chance to complete the final pieces of the puzzle.

Part II
"The enemy is fear. We think it is hate; but it is fear."

Mohandas Karamchand Ghandi

October 1943

By the time they reached the top of the mountain pass, Liesi, who was still recovering from the wounds sustained in the bombing, needed to rest. She put her pack under her head and lay back in exhaustion. Magda was concerned for their safety and kept watch. When a muffled sound startled her, she felt her body stiffen to alertness. Someone was coming! They were in an open area and she looked around frantically for a place to hide. However, there was nothing but low scrub and small rocks in sight. Liesi was in no condition to either run or fight. Magda knew she would have to defend them both. Her backpack was the heaviest object at hand so she eased it from her shoulders and grasped the strap firmly with her two fists. She was crouched in that position when a German soldier stepped onto the summit. He seemed as surprised as she was and his rifle was not raised so she took advantage and lunged at him. With all the strength she could muster, she swung the pack over her head and gave him a solid whack. He lost his balance and fell backward. She heard a dull 'thunk' as his head hit a rock, and then he lay still. She inched near and saw that, though he was breathing, he was out cold. Her mind raced for ideas on how to restrain him. Eyeing some rope looped around his belt, she crept up to him and began to undo it with trembling hands. She rolled him over, tied his wrists behind his back and then looped the rest of it around his ankles. After that, she took a scarf from her head and made it into a gag for his mouth. When she was finished, she couldn't believe that she had the nerve and strength to do it. There was no time to rest, however. Even more terrifying was the possibility that he had comrades in the vicinity that might discover them. She knew that their only hope of survival was to hide him and somehow get herself and Liesi to Herr König.

That returned her thoughts to Liesi. She pulled back from the soldier and glanced across at her friend. She was in a deep sleep and the moonlight seemed to emphasize how ill and vulnerable she was.

Magda's own legs were shaking so much that she could barely walk but she knew that she had to move the soldier out of sight. There was no way that she could lift him and he was even too heavy to drag. If she could just roll his body a short distance, the flat area fell off quickly. Using his rifle as a lever, she tried to shift him. Even using all of the strength she had left, the task was slow and she was drenched with perspiration by the time momentum took over. It was almost surreal to see him disappear over the side and into the brush but the reality of the situation and her desire to stay alive, drew her back to Liesi and the daunting task of getting her off the mountain.

Liesi was beginning to come around and Magda signaled for her to be silent because stealth was important until they were safely away from the Austrian border. She leaned close and whispered, "We have to get out of here. Do you think you have the strength to move if I support you?" Liesi nodded but then almost passed out as she tried to sit up. Nevertheless, she gritted her teeth, forced herself upright, and leaned hard on her friend's shoulder. The two began a slow shuffle down the other side of the mountain and their fear was eased somewhat by Magda's possession of the soldier's rifle.

Chapter 29 — A Fateful Night

I tossed and turned much of the night but managed a few hours of sleep. As I wake up, I'm agitated, not just from the restless night, but also from the new dream about Liesi and Magda. They had a very scary encounter with a German soldier at the Austrian-Swiss border. I feel new respect for the difficulty they went through to get to *Herr* König's safe house. As astonishing as the dream information is, I decide to keep it to myself for the time being. I want to hear what else Doctor Martin has to say and see if my dream matches up with his facts. I guess you could say that I'm testing my skills. I do take the time to tell my diary that 'Gisela' was Liesi.

Christoph and Sigrid Falke
great, great grandparents (built Haus Falke)

Dr. Anna (Falke) Schumann   *Elizabeth (Liesi) Falke*
great grandma (Uroma)   *(Gisela von Werz)*
                                  (died 1946)
                                  Johann König?

Dr. Sabine Müller   *Christoph König*
grandma (Oma)   *(son-died 2008)*

Silke Hofstetter (m. Franz)   *Lukas König (grandson)*
Parents

Sebastian (Basti) & Annika

Since *Frau* Petra König requested that we meet while her son Lukas is at his sport club for soccer training, our group leaves for Innsbrück quite early this morning.

Basti and I each had mini panic attacks when both sets of parents hesitated to give their consents last night. First we approached my parents because I figured they would be supportive and then we could use that to convince Basti's parents. Their reaction wasn't quite what I had hoped.

Dad said, "Ellen, I know that this is important to you and we have no problem with you going to Innsbrück with Basti and Anna. Hopefully the meeting will provide all of the answers you are seeking. However, if things aren't finished then, you will have to keep in touch long distance because our flights on Saturday are set and it will be expensive to change the reservations for four people."

Talk about pressure! I crossed my fingers and toes and prayed for no complications. We talked to Basti's parents next. *Herr* Hofstetter exploded. *"Wieder zu Innsbrück? Nein!"*

Nein means *no* and Basti and I looked at one another in panic. Basti pleaded, *"Papa, bitte."*

Luckily, *Uroma* Anna heard the commotion and she came downstairs. Her calm voice said, *"Hör mal, Franz."* She was asking him to listen.

In German, she said, "I am at the end of my life, Franz. This is my last chance to find out what happened to my sister Liesi. I am going and I would like for Basti to come with me. Please."

"Anna, this trip is too much for you! I worry."

"Franz, not knowing is too much for me!"

In the end, *Herr* Hofstetter couldn't say no and, when the Grübers come to pick us up, the three of us are ready and waiting.

In the car, we're all very quiet, partly due to the early hour and maybe because we all have our own concerns about how the visit will play out. I'm worried that I won't hear the full story before Saturday and I'm dying to find out if my dream is true.

Doktor Erika breaks the silence. "Martin, are you feeling okay? If at any time this is too much, just tell me and I will turn around."

"I'm fine. And even if I weren't, I want to do this for Magda. When she made the trip to Austria last July, despite her illness, she never got to tell Liesi's family the story. Luckily, she did tell John enough for him to pass it on to me. It took a lot of courage but then my father always said she had courage. I promised John that I would finish her mission..." His voice trails off and somehow we all know that he needs time alone with his thoughts. For the rest of the ride, we're all quiet.

Doktor Erika's silver Mercedes crosses the bridge over the Inn River and enters the city of Innsbrück just before 9 am. *Frau* Petra greets us with warmth but her face cannot completely mask the tension. She guides us to the dining room table where a fresh-baked *Apfelkuchen* lies waiting, and then she busies herself retrieving fresh-brewed *Kaffee*, milk and juice from the kitchen. With nervous hands, she pours the drinks, cuts the cake and fusses over us. When everyone is taken care of, she takes a deep breath, as if preparing herself for whatever she is about to learn.

I'm not very hungry. I just sip some juice, anxious for the rest of the story to begin. I notice that Basti is only picking at his *Apfelkuchen*.

I whisper in his ear, "Are you okay?"

He nods but he doesn't look at me and I notice that he is holding his Uroma Anna's arm.

Frau Petra sits down, places her hands on the table with fingers entwined, and squares her shoulders. She nods at Doctor Martin to signal she is ready. All eyes are riveted on him as he begins. He again apologizes for his lack of good German language skills but says that Doctor Erika has offered to translate for *Frau* Petra's sake. We soon hear the two of them take turns telling a bilingual tale.

"*Frau* Petra, the story I am about to tell may seem puzzling to you at first so I ask for your patience. In the end, I believe that you will see the significance."

He begins the tale of "Ute" and "Gisela" that John MacDougal told him, as well as the key bit of information he heard from Magda herself — the fact that they were Magda and Liesi.

I've heard some of the escape story before so I don't pay close attention until I hear the following words: "With new Swiss IDs, Magda Alt and Liesi Falke set off by night over the mountains via an old smuggler's path from Ischgl, Austria toward Switzerland as Ute Seidl and Gisela von Werz. They were heading for the last link in the chain, *Herr* Johann König in Samnaun."

Basti interrupts saying, "That may be the same route you took, Ellen Troy!"

Doctor Martin says, "It was very dangerous then because the borders were patrolled by Nazi soldiers. Switzerland was the last neutral country in central Europe and a place of refuge for people fleeing Nazi persecution."

I nod and then just wait for him to tell about the mountaintop struggle. However, all he says is that they had a narrow escape from a Nazi soldier.

Okay. I can't keep my mouth shut and I blurt out, "You didn't mention the details, Doctor Martin and that was the scariest part."

Doctor Martin's eyes widen and his voice sounds uneasy.

"Ellen, how do you know what was scary?"

I feel a bit like an alien creature but I need to say it.

"I had a dream last night."

"Are you saying that your dream showed you what happened on that mountain?"

All at once, I'm aware that everyone in the room is staring at me like I'm a bug under a microscope but there's no turning back.

I murmur, "I… I think so."

Doctor Martin's brow furrows but Basti's voice breaks the silence.

"Go ahead, Ellen Troy."

I look at him and smile, take a deep breath, and plunge ahead.

"Magda knocked him out with her backpack, tied him up and rolled him into the brush."

There is complete silence until Doctor Martin whispers, "Ellen, I can't believe you know these details!"

A chorus of surprised comments surrounds me, and Doctor Martin is shaking his head.

I look him in the eye and say, "It's good to know I didn't just imagine it."

The room is quiet again and I have the feeling that I may have just freaked everyone out a little bit. I can't worry about that now. Before Doctor Martin resumes his story, I have to ask one more question. "One thing bugs me. Switzerland is small and Nazi-occupied countries surrounded it. How could such a tiny country keep the Nazis from invading it when the big ones couldn't?"

Doctor Martin says, "If I remember correctly from a class in college, it was because the Germans needed resources that Switzerland had."

In a quiet voice, *Uroma* Anna adds something in German and Basti translates. "It was also because the Swiss military were against Hitler and would have given him more trouble than losing its resources was worth. She also says that is not what we came to discuss. Can we please get back to Liesi and Magda's story?"

Oops. I feel bad for interrupting and I apologize to her, *"Es tut mir leid, Frau Doktor Schumann."*

Doctor Martin continues, "What happened on that mountain peak haunted Magda." Then he pauses and asks for some water.

I glance over at Basti, and I see that he has his arm around *Uroma* Anna. I can only imagine how terrifying it is for her to hear this about her only sister and her friend. It's hard for me and I didn't even know them.

As we wait, no one says anything but I'm guessing we're all worried about what he hasn't yet told us — how and when Liesi died.

Chapter 30 — Ties That Bind

No one says a word during the pause, but Doctor Martin soon brings us back to that mountainside.

"By dawn, the women were close to the bottom of the mountain but they didn't want to draw attention to themselves by walking into town in daylight. Switzerland was a free country but some people opposed the increasing numbers of refugees and how they might deplete the already scarce food rations. So they looked for a sheltered spot to stop and pretty much collapsed when they found one. Exhaustion soon gave way to sleep and it was afternoon before either of them woke up."

Doctor Martin stops and takes a sip of his water before continuing.

"They waited for darkness, pushed forward once again and, at last, made their way to *Herr* König's door. The first thing that he did was to call a *Doktor*. A thorough examination revealed that 'Gisela' was weak and exhausted but her wounds were clean and not infected.

Uroma Anna's voice shouts, *"Gott sei dank!"* It means *Thank God*.

Doctor Martin doesn't look quite so relieved. His face is unreadable as he continues.

"Both women were cared for in the König's home and given time to regain their strength. When they improved, both of them found work as assistants in a medical clinic and soon were busy with war victims. Switzerland was filled with imprisoned French and Polish troops, downed Allied aircraft crews, German and Italian deserters, escaped prisoners of war, and a variety of civilian refugees, including Jews who had arrived before the 'J' stamp was introduced."

"Excuse me for interrupting, Doctor Martin, but may I ask a question?"

"Of course, Ellen. Go ahead."

"What was a 'J' stamp?"

"The Nazis made it mandatory for the passports of all Jewish people to be stamped with a red 'J', Ellen."

"That's like branding them!"

"Yes, and once this happened, officials in Switzerland prohibited entry to anyone with this Jewish stamp."

I feel sick to my stomach because it's not just branding, it's a death sentence. All I can manage to say though is, "That's so wrong!"

"You've got that right, Ellen, and it's just one of millions of nasty atrocities Jewish people suffered at that time."

The room is silent until Doctor Martin says, "Let me get back to the clinic because it's important to Liesi and Magda's story. As I was saying, many of these people needed medical attention and came to the clinic. Several weeks after 'Ute' and 'Gisela's' work began, a young man came into the clinic suffering from a bullet wound to his calf."

Uroma Anna seems impatient and says, "Please, just tell us about Liesi and Magda, Doctor Martin!"

"I assure you that this man is important to their story, *Frau Doktor* Schumann. Please bear with me."

Her look is doubtful but she nods.

"The man was Swiss but was brought in by a Frenchman that *Herr* König knew to be active in the Resistance against the Nazis. As 'Gisela' assisted in dressing the wound, she asked him what happened. He smiled and teased, 'I just wanted to be nursed by a pretty girl.' Evidently 'Gisela' blushed and seemed disappointed when he limped away. He didn't stay away though. He came back a week later and said that he wanted her to know that she healed his leg but caused him pain in his heart."

"She didn't fall for that cheesy line, did she?"

"She must have, Ellen. It was the beginning of a whirlwind courtship. Within months, they married and it wasn't long before they were expecting a child."

Basti seems fired up as he asks, "Liesi married someone she barely knew?"

Doctor Martin explains, "You have to understand that it was wartime, Basti. They both probably realized that danger could grab happiness away from them in a flash."

It bothers me too so I say, "But she hardly trusted anybody because of the Nazis!"

"Well, Ellen, Magda told me that he would often disappear on secret missions. The idea of him being part of the Resistance against the Nazis may have added to the attraction she felt for him."

I say no more but, for some reason, I have a bad feeling about this. I look at Basti and I can tell that it still bothers him too.

With a soft voice, *Uroma* Anna asks, "Was this marriage a happy time for my Liesi?"

Doctor Martin's face clouds and he answers, "I'm sorry to say that her happiness was short-lived, *Frau Schumann.*"

He takes a deep breath and locks eyes with Uroma Anna. His voice softens and he grabs onto both of her hands, as if to share his strength.

"She had a difficult pregnancy and felt ill much of the time. Then midway through the nine months, tragedy struck; her husband went missing while on a mission."

Uroma Anna's intake of breath is audible.

Doctor Martin's eyes are glistening now as tells her, "Her health declined even more and the birth was difficult. As she held her son for the first time, Liesi knew that she was dying and she lived only four more days."

Uroma Anna sways and her voice reacts with a soulful, *"Mein Gott!"*

Doctor Martin waits a beat and then says, "Liesi made Magda promise several things."

Uroma Anna seems to gain strength and asks, "What were the promises, Doctor Martin?"

"The first was that her child was to be named Christoph."

This time, *Frau* Petra reacts, "My Christoph?"

Doctor Martin says, "Yes, *Frau* Petra, and he was named after Liesi's beloved father and as a tribute to the bravery of her former classmate, Christoph Probst, who was executed by the Nazis."

I notice tears rolling down *Frau* Petra's cheeks as she whispers, "If he only knew…"

Doctor Martin pauses a moment and then says, "Magda also promised to take over Christoph's care if his papa was never found and to see that he was embraced by whatever family Liesi had remaining in *München* after the war."

I fight back tears as Doctor Martin takes another sip of water. I feel like I've opened a wound in Uroma Anna's heart. In the quiet, she is sobbing as she whispers once more, *"Mein Gott!"*

My heart goes out to her. She always assumed that her sister Liesi died but hearing the heartbreaking circumstances of her death must be a shock. Basti seems to be holding on to her more tightly and his own face is pale. I want to go over and sit beside him to give him support but the mystery solver in me has to ask, "Doctor Martin, if Liesi and her husband were his parents, why wasn't Christoph given his papa's last name? Also, if Magda promised to take care of him, how did he come to be named König?"

Doctor Martin smiles and says, "Very good observation, Ellen. 'Ute', that is, Magda, told her husband, John, that Christoph was given his papa's last name at first and she did try to fulfill her promises. However, his papa didn't return and, more and more, she found herself relying on the Königs for the baby's care. In the end, she had no means to raise a child herself and realized that the Königs loved him as their own."

Uroma Anna seems upset and asks, "But why didn't Magda keep her promise to find my parents so they would know their grandson?"

"When the war ended, she did try, *Frau* Schumann but finding people in the postwar chaos and rubble of the city was difficult at best, as I'm sure you must remember."

"But we never left *München*!"

"You must understand that Magda was only twenty-four years old and alone, with little income and even less time. The thought of returning to Germany at that time, even if she had the means, frightened her because she wasn't sure how her false identity papers would be viewed by the occupying forces. Plus, where would she have gone? She had learned that her family's house was destroyed and her mother was dead."

Magda's abandonment of the baby bothers me. "So, why didn't she just stay with the baby at the Königs until things got better, Doctor Martin?"

"Food rationing was still in effect then, Ellen, and she could no longer justify being a burden to the Königs. She needed to support herself but the Samnaun clinic pay wasn't enough. So, *Herr* König made inquiries and found that the International Red Cross desperately needed help in Zurich and the pay was good."

"Well. If she could make more money, she could have supported the baby, right?"

"Ellen, as the Königs pointed out to her, though she had agreed to her friend's dying wish, there was no reasonable way to make it happen at that moment. The pay in Zurich would not be enough to pay for childcare and she would need that while she was at work. As for Liesi's family, it might take years to find them, and the longer it took, the harder it would be for the child. The Königs loved Christoph and he now thought of them as his mama and papa. They wanted to adopt him and give him a loving and stable home."

It sinks in that she tried to do the best for Christoph and I say so, "I guess it was a really hard decision for Magda."

"Exactly, Ellen. The Königs didn't rush her and she put off the decision for some time but in the end, she felt it was the best solution for all, given the circumstances. She agreed to the adoption but also demanded a promise; some day the Königs must allow her to tell Christoph the truth about his biological mother."

Something else is still bothering me. Why didn't she also want to tell Christoph about his biological father? It seems odd to me but, for the time being, I say nothing. Instead I ask, "So, Doctor Martin, Magda didn't keep one of her promises because she thought it was best for the baby but why did it take her so long to keep the promise of telling him the truth?"

"Ah, Ellen, I can see why you solve old mysteries. You are persistent about getting to the heart of each problem. I guess the short answer is that life got in the way. The longer answer shows how complicated that life was and it will take a little while to explain. Why don't we all take a short break and then I will pass on what Magda's husband, John, told me, okay?"

Chapter 31 — Aborted Connections

During the break, I sit next to Basti and ask how he's doing. He just shrugs and takes my hand. *Uroma* Anna reaches from his other side and places her hand over the both of ours and gently squeezes. None of us seem to have words for what is transpiring.

When Doctor Martin resumes his explanation, he says, "I think Magda's delay in keeping her promise was due to her own problems at first. Through her work in Zurich, she met her husband, John MacDougal. He was a U.S. Army corporal and he fell in love with 'Ute Seidl.' Despite the U.S. objections toward marriages with German-speaking nationals at that time, John fought for them. She wanted to tell him the truth about her identity but worried that it would jeopardize their relationship and their case. Their marriage and her eventual emigration to California involved a lot of red tape and in all of the documents she was identified as Ute Seidl MacDougal. Magdalena Alt had become another lifetime."

"Okay, but, why couldn't she fulfill her promise as Ute MacDougal?"

"Magda said that she never forgot her promise, Ellen, but she put it on the back burner for some years. Her life became pretty busy after moving to America. She finished her medical education, developed her practice, and had two daughters with John."

"Did she ever try?"

"Yes. Years later, she finally wrote to the Königs. However, they begged for more time. They said that Christoph was happy and doing well and the thought of upsetting his secure world at such a young age was unbearable to them. She told them that she would come when they were ready."

"So she left it up to the Königs to decide? Why?"

"Well, I suppose it gave her an excuse to put off telling her own family. She knew that if they learned about Christoph and Liesi, it might lead to revelations about her own former life and she was afraid of the possible consequences."

Basti sounds angry when he speaks, "So, Magda put her own interests before Christoph's?!"

"Well, Basti, even though the Königs' request made the decision to wait easier, didn't she owe the Königs the right to decide when to tell Christoph?"

Basti doesn't look convinced but he says nothing.

I decide to switch the focus, "So what did make Magda finally decide to tell Christoph, Doctor Martin?"

"Many years later, she received a letter from *Herr* König, Ellen. She said that she stared at the envelope without opening it for many minutes, knowing that her promises were past due. She wondered if he had finally decided it was time for her to tell Christoph. The letter itself began as a death announcement and ended as a soul bearing of sorts. *Herr* König's dear wife, Helga, had recently died and he was beside himself with grief but also filled with regret. Many years before, he had pushed their son too hard to go to university and Christoph had felt misunderstood and alienated. At the age of eighteen, Christoph left home and never looked back."

I can't help but think that some kids would give anything to have the chance to go to college and I wonder why Christoph didn't want to go. I don't say it though.

"Helga was devastated and urged her husband to go after the boy and reconcile. However, *Herr* König was too proud, angry and hurt. After Helga died, he felt guilty about depriving her of Christoph's presence in her final years. He also began to wonder if they had done the right thing keeping the secret of Christoph's adoption from him. For years, they told one another that they wanted to protect him from some ugly truths, but the reality was that they also feared Christoph's love for them would change."

Though I think Christoph did have the right to know he was adopted, I'm curious what these "ugly truths" could be. Could they be related to his mysterious biological father or am I jumping to conclusions? I hold these thoughts and hope that Doctor Martin will eventually explain.

"*Herr* König had learned that his son was living in Innsbrück and decided to tell him the truth about his birth as well as to ask forgiveness for the deception. With 'Ute's' permission, he wanted to enclose the locket that she had entrusted to him all those years before containing Liesi's 'Wolfgang' photo. Christoph wouldn't be able to discern her lovely face behind the mask but perhaps her eyes would be a comfort? If she agreed, he would give 'Ute's' address to Christoph and leave it to his son's discretion whether to contact her or not.

"'Ute' had been overcome with all kinds of emotions and had written back a letter of condolence, comfort, and permission. However, she heard nothing from Christoph so she continued to focus on her California life and family."

"Doctor Martin, if Christoph never contacted her, what made her go to Austria?"

"Her own diagnosis of incurable cancer made her decide, Ellen. She wanted to fulfill her promise before she died. Tragically, her health didn't allow that to happen."

Uroma Anna says, "Knowing that she was so sick, how could her husband let her make the trip?"

"She never told him, *Frau* Schumann. He thought they were taking a vacation. When she collapsed during the trip, he learned the truth. After that, she also told him about Christoph and Liesi, but left out some details about herself. She still worried that her deception would hurt him."

"So she's dead and he still doesn't know who she really was?"

"Sadly, yes, Ellen."

Turning to *Frau* Petra, Doctor Martin says, "Magda made the phone call to Innsbrück in August and found you by pure determination. When she could find no phone listing for Christoph, she tried the only other König who was listed in the city. Upon learning that Christoph had died, she came to the conclusion that she had failed to keep her promise. However, since I was able to tell her husband, John, about Christoph's son (thanks to Ellen and Basti), he asked me to explain the truth to Lukas and to help him meet his birth family. Though it's too late for Christoph, he feels that informing Lukas fulfills his wife's promise — at least in part. I gave my word to try and, *Frau* Petra, I hope that you will give your permission."

Chapter 32 — Perspectives

When Doctor Martin finishes, the room is quiet. Each person absorbs the information and contemplates the impact from his or her own perspective.

Frau Petra König has tears in her eyes as she speaks, "This story explains so much about my ex-husband's secretive and angry life. Whenever I tried to broach the subject of Christoph's childhood with him, he shut me down. In the beginning of our relationship, his personality was aggressive but, at times, he was also very compassionate. Later on, his hotheaded nature won out most of the time. It saddens me to think that his impulsiveness cut him off from the very caring people who might have saved him from more pain."

Her words then reflect on her son. "Lukas knows very little about his papa's early life and nothing about his grandparents. Both he and Christoph assumed that their real family name was König though. I think it's important that Lukas learns who he is and where he comes from."

Uroma Anna's voice is shaky but her words show strength. "I am in shock hearing of my sister's ordeal but I must focus on the next steps. I have just learned of the existence of my grand nephew, Liesi's grandson, and I thank you, *Frau* Petra, for agreeing to let him meet my family. I would also like to visit Samnaun to pay respects to my sister and the Königs who took her in and loved her and her child. Finally, I must decide if Liesi's remains should come home to *München*, stay near the Königs, or rest with her son in Innsbrück. I very much want to do what is right but the choices are many and, right now, I must admit that I am exhausted just thinking about them."

Doktor Erika looks around at the profound effect her cousin's words have had on the gathering and smiles as she says, "I feel a renewed admiration for my *Oncle* Heribert's wartime efforts. Like many German young people, I have been burdened with guilt for the actions of my elders. My *Oncle* has made me proud to bear the name Grüber. It's a rare occurrence for a modern German to be able to feel pride for the past. Though what my *Oncle* did was a small gesture in the scheme of things, it took courage and moral strength during a horrific time. Maybe his efforts didn't directly save anyone from the gas chambers, but they did help to keep more German children from being brainwashed with the poisonous Nazi philosophy. I'm grateful for that."

Looking at Basti, I can see that he is deep in thought and seems very sad. I'm reminded that this whole mystery is very personal to him. I'm also reminded that I'm leaving for the States in the morning and I'm not ready to say good-bye to this heart-friend and collaborator who has made my year in Germany so memorable. I feel weighted down with sadness too but not just because I will miss him. This whole experience has left me feeling drained. I've worked so hard to solve this mystery but Liesi didn't survive as I had hoped and it's too late to meet Magda. I shake myself and try to focus on the positives. We *did* find Doctor Martin, the son of *Doktor* Heribert Grüber who organized both the resistance work and the escape plan. He followed our clues to locate Magda in California and confirm that it was Liesi's body in Gisela's grave. However, I want to know how it will be resolved with Lukas and to visit Samnaun for some real closure. Call me crazy but I have a nagging feeling that this mystery hasn't completely unfolded.

Chapter 33 — Grave Implications

Uroma Anna's voice pierces my thoughts, "*Frau* Petra, I would very much like to meet Lukas when he returns today."

Everyone in the room looks at *Frau* Petra. It's a moment before she speaks but, when she does, she lays out some ground rules. "I would like for you all to meet my Lukas but I would prefer to break the news to him in private. He's due home at about 13:30. I will give him lunch and prepare him for your visit. If you can come back at about 14:30, you may tell him the details of his grandmother's life."

Uroma Anna thanks her and Doctor Martin suggests that the rest of us take a lunch break. The mystery of Liesi's husband is still nagging at me though and I decide to finally ask, "Doctor Martin, didn't Magda tell you who Liesi's husband was? That might be important for Lukas to know, right?"

He looks startled and then sad. "As I've said before Ellen, you always seem to get to the nitty-gritty. How could I have forgotten one of the most important but unfortunate details?"

Frau Petra reacts as if she's stung. "What do you mean *unfortunate*?"

Doctor Martin seems to steady himself and then explains. "John MacDougal never learned his name but, after 'Gisela's' death, it was revealed that her husband had been captured working for the Nazis as a double agent. He was tried and convicted and died years later in prison. That's why they didn't put her married name on the gravestone."

Frau Petra's immediate reaction is, "My son is too young to have to know that! To tell him that his grandfather was a Nazi spy is out of the question! All he needs to know is that his grandfather was a Swiss soldier killed in the war."

I can't believe what I'm hearing and I speak my mind. "He may be only twelve years old but that's old enough to realize that her friend Magda would have known who his grandfather was!"

Doctor Martin doesn't seem to like my outburst and says, "The boy doesn't need to have all of the nasty facts, Ellen. If Lukas asks any questions, we should point out how confusing the war years were and how trauma may have affected Magda's memory."

I can't believe my ears. I was twelve years old myself only three years ago and I'm pretty sure I wouldn't have bought that story. With my mouth hanging open, I look toward Basti for support but he just shrugs.

Doctor Martin stands up, thanks our hostess and heads for the exit, promising to return at 14:30. I have no choice but to follow his lead.

When we're all outside, Doctor Martin suggests that we have lunch at a well-known inn, the *Goldener Adler*, his treat. *Doktor* Erika and *Uroma* Anna seem pleased but Basti can see that I'm out of sorts. He asks if he and I might go off on our own for something more casual, like a Currywurst or pizza. The grownups are reluctant at first but he promises that we'll be trustworthy and will meet them on time, so they cave.

Once we're on our own, he doesn't say anything for a while. He seems to need some space and so do I. When he stops in front of a gyro place, he asks me if that sounds ok. I nod and we go inside. We eat in silence for a while and then I ask, "Basti, what were your first thoughts after Doctor Martin finished his story?"

"I was thinking that Lukas and I are part of the same family but I'm not sure what you'd call our relationship. He is a grandnephew to *Uroma* Anna and *Oma* Sabine would be his second cousin, I think. Am I his 4th cousin or something, and does that even matter? I wonder if Lukas will become part of my life now and if I will like him. We're close in age but will we have anything in common? Does that sound selfish?"

"No, it sounds normal. Besides, you are one of the least selfish people I know, Basti. You've given up a lot of your own plans in order to help me this year. I appreciate that."

A crooked smile forms on his face. *"Na jah,* it sometimes surprises me how I believed you, followed you, and joined in your quest... but I haven't regretted a single minute. When you leave, the days will seem dull and ordinary."

I blush. I don't quite know what to say but I think, *Wow!* When I do manage to find my voice, I change the subject. "You know what I'd like to do, Basti? I'd like to visit Christoph's grave. I have a feeling he wants to talk to us."

Basti almost spits out his cola so I can obviously still surprise him. Wiping his mouth with a paper napkin, he looks at me and recognizes the determination. He knows better than to fight it. "I guess we might have time to do that if he is buried in the city. I wonder where we might find out?"

Just then, there's a fluttering sound at the window behind him and my eyes light up. "Don't worry. Our guide has just arrived."

"A crow?"

"Of course."

"Just because a crow guided you and Manon in Samnaun doesn't mean that every crow has that power, Ellen Troy!"

"Trust me."

We head down an alley where the black crow has flown, believing that it will turn up again when we come to a crossroads. Sure enough, we find it sitting on a curb at the first intersection. It takes off again to the right.

At the next intersection, we're momentarily perplexed because the bird is nowhere to be seen. Then hearing a *whoosh,* we look up to see it land on the top of a signpost. There are a number of sites listed, each followed by an arrow and a certain amount of kilometers. The third one down says, *Friedhof — 2 kilometer* and the arrow points straight ahead. *Friedhof* means *cemetery* and two kilometers is only a little over a mile. Easy peasy. Our excitement starts to mount and we begin to run. Our heartbeats speed up to keep pace with our swift-moving feet.

We're panting when we reach the gate to the cemetery but we don't stop for long. Searching the sky, we catch sight of the black wings and walk inside toward the area where the bird has landed. We don't speak, as we are each now focused on the path that leads toward our goal.

Then, there it is! It's a simple stone that lies flat on the ground. There are no designs or ornaments. It simply states, *Christoph Lukas König, 1946–2008.*

Basti is disappointed and says so. "Is this all there is? We've run all the way for nothing!" Addressing the stone he says, "What's the matter, *Herr* Christoph? Have you changed your mind about talking?" He looks at me expecting a comment but I'm lost in my own world of thought. I'm concentrating on the words and say nothing for many minutes. Basti knows better than to interrupt me when I get like this so he goes silent and waits.

"What is it about this inscription, Basti, that you didn't expect to see?"

The sound of my voice piercing the silence rouses him from his own reflections. He says that it looks pretty normal then adds, "But then, I guess I didn't know that Lukas was given his papa's middle…"

"Exactly! The name *Lukas* is the surprise!" Warming up to my own idea, I take it further. "We were brought here to see the name Lukas. So… Lukas… the young Lukas… must hold the key to whatever mystery still awaits!"

Basti looks at me with a mixture of frustration and disbelief. This time, he believes that I have taken a leap of faith or intuition or whatever too far. He's tired and cranky and lets it show in his words. "You are crazy this time, Ellen Troy! What makes you even think that there is any more mystery to be solved? You have put all the pieces together that can be put together. Now your job is finished and I think, after we meet Lukas, we have to move on." With that said, he adds, "If we're to be back at the König's on time, we should get going." He turns on his heel and begins the trek back to town.

I run to catch up, but not before thanking Christoph.

Chapter 34 — Lukas

He joins us at the dining room table without speaking and without making eye contact. In fact, *uncomfortable* is the word that comes to mind when I look at Lukas. Petra König rests her hand on her son's shoulder in a gesture of support but she seems anxious herself.

Doctor Martin clears his throat and extends his hand. The boy seems reluctant but accepts it as the doctor introduces himself, again with Doctor Erika translating.

"Lukas, my name is Martin Grüber. I think you will be proud to know that your grandmother was a brave woman with whom my father was privileged to work during wartime. If not for her and for a few others, more young German children would have been made into followers of Hitler."

The boy's face registers little emotion but Doctor Martin keeps going. "This lovely lady sitting next to me is your grandmother's sister. I would like you to meet *Frau Doktor* Anna Falke Schumann."

Like a robot, Lukas extends his hand to *Uroma* Anna for the expected polite handshake. She startles him by dispensing with formality and grasping his hand in both of hers. Warmth floods from her. *"Mein Gott! Du bist meine Familie. Du kommst von meine Liesi."* She then tells him about his grandmother Liesi, about his great-grandparents, Christoph and Sigrid Falke, her own daughter Sabine, and her granddaughter Silke. Turning to her left and giving Basti's arm an affectionate squeeze, she introduces him. She adds that, if it were not for Basti and his American friend, me, (whom she acknowledges with a wink) his grandmother would never have been found. And, of course, we would never have had the pleasure of meeting him, Liesi's only grandson. *Uroma* Anna seems beside herself with joy and excitement but, still, the boy is unresponsive.

There's dead silence until I nudge Basti and he makes an attempt at conversation. He speaks in simple German, confident that I will be able to understand the drift, if not the entirety. He says that he has something in common with Lukas's papa; his own middle name is Christoph, in honor of his great-grandfather, Christoph Falke. "I believe that your papa was named for him too. After all, he was his grandson."

All eyes focus on Lukas and when he realizes that an answer is expected, he manages to mumble, "Yes."

Again, the silence is deafening. This time I whisper something to Basti and he asks another question that is very direct. "Who are *you* named for, Lukas?"

Lukas blinks and recoils as if fielding a hardball. His mother notices this and answers for him. "He is named after his papa whose middle name was Lukas, and his middle name is Erich for *my* grandfather."

A hint of sorrow shows on Lukas's face. "You forgot my other name, mother — my confirmation name."

Frau Petra shakes her head and says that she should have remembered that one, since they had disagreed. "I had always loved *Sankt* Josef and Josef was also my papa's name so I encouraged him to choose that. He got very upset which was quite unlike him. Instead, he wanted to choose

Johann, his other grandfather's name. It is a good saint's name but I couldn't imagine why he would choose the name of a grandfather he had never met over one who had held him as a baby! In the end, he chose to please his *Mutti* and he agreed to the name Josef. He is a good son, my Lukas."

Something about the sorrowful look spurs me to action and I blurt out my question in English. "Is there a bad association with the name Josef for you, Lukas?"

Basti looks like he can't believe what I have just asked but he translates my words anyway.

"Nein!" The denial comes from Petra before Lukas has a chance to answer.

In German, Lukas says, *"Mutti,* will you please stop answering for me? I am not a child! Papa was the same way. He always treated me like a child who should be kept in a bubble of innocence!" Looking at me, he says that he understood my question without translation, because he is learning English at school. However, he needs to continue to speak in German, so his mother can understand.

I nod and urge him to continue and I realize that I've struck a nerve. His once unemotional features seem to animate as pent up feelings come to the surface. "My papa had so many secrets but wouldn't tell me anything! My grandfather, who I now know is my adoptive grandfather, was said to be mean. Now I know he was not. My papa always pretended to be honest but, in my heart, I knew he wasn't a legitimate businessman! My papa had learned who his birth parents were but he wouldn't tell me that either! They were my family too! I had a right to know!"

Something he said catches my attention. "Did you say birth *parents*? We thought he only learned about his mother."

Lukas seems to gain some inner strength and, for the first time, looks defiant. "I told my mother that Papa had thrown the letter from Johann König into the fireplace. That was true but only in part. There had been no fire. What I also didn't say was that the letter contained an object and it was thrown into the fireplace with the letter. I was only six but the words he spoke as he flung them chilled me — 'Go to hell, Papa!'"

At this point, *Frau* Petra looks pale and we're all riveted.

Lukas continues, "When Papa calmed down, he seemed to have second thoughts. He reached into the hearth and retrieved both items. As he dusted them off, he was deep in thought. Then he took the letter and the second object and put them into an envelope and sealed it. He wrote my name on the outside and then sat me down. He said that I wouldn't understand what was in the envelope then but, when I was older, it was going to tell me a very important thing that might even save my life some day. He said that he would hold onto it until he thought I could handle it and then we could read it together."

Frau Petra whispers, "Lukas, why didn't you tell me?"

"I was just happy to have a secret to share with Papa, *Mutti.* After he died, I went to his house on my own and found the envelope. Then I hid it in my room. I decided to open it on my tenth birthday, thinking that double numbers made me old enough to handle whatever it held. I was hardly prepared. The letter was from Johann and it explained that Papa was adopted when he was a baby because both of his parents had died in the war. It also explained that his mother was a good woman from *München* who had been wounded while escaping from the Nazis and that she died after giving birth while living in his house. She had named my papa Christoph Lukas — Christoph after her father and a brave friend and Lukas after the patron saint of doctors. Her real name was Elisabeth Beatrix Falke but she was buried under her cover name of Gisela von Werz. My grandfather, on the other hand, was described as a man who had seemed honorable and who said he loved my grandmother. After they married however, he disappeared while thought to be working undercover fighting the Nazis. My grandmother died thinking that he was a hero. Johann later learned that he was a Nazi double agent who was arrested and convicted. He died in prison. He said that he was reluctant to reveal this horror to my papa but felt it was important to know birth family history in case of sickness. I guess that's what Papa meant about it possibly saving my life. After reading the letter, I picked up the other object — a marriage certificate for Gisela von Werz and her husband. The name of the papa he had told to go to hell was in my hands… Josef Gottfried Eicke."

Lukas turns to his mother, who now has tears running down her cheeks, and says, "Forgive me, *Mutti,* but after that, every time I heard the name Josef I was filled with the shame of my grandfather's actions. When I was picking my confirmation name and you suggested Josef, I was repulsed. I wanted to tell you why but you already had such bad memories of Papa, I didn't want to give you another reason to hate him."

Petra reaches for her son and draws him into her arms. "Oh my poor boy. You shouldn't have had to carry this burden all by yourself. Your papa may have left some bad memories but I could never hate him. After all, he gave me you, my wonderful son."

Lukas's shoulders seem to relax, as if shedding a heavy weight. After a few moments of shelter in his mother's arms however, he pulls free and looks at the rest of us. "I worried at first about those nasty genes that my real grandfather passed along, especially since Papa was no angel. However, I've come to realize that, in the end, Papa listened to his good adoptive papa and thought about my protection. It showed me that people can learn to be better if they have good examples around them. I just wish that my

Nazi grandfather had opened his heart to better examples. It was rare but not impossible in Hitler's Germany, I think. Your papa, *Herr Doktor* Grüber, was living proof of that and I thank him for my grandmother."

Wow! For a twelve year old, I think this kid is pretty impressive.

With promises to stay in touch, *Uroma* Anna hugs Lukas and *Frau* Petra and then, with tears in her eyes, hugs Basti and me and tells us that we did good work.

Emotions are high as we all say goodbye and head out to the car for the long ride back to Munich.

Chapter 35 — Memories

As *Doktor* Erika maneuvers her car back through the streets of Innsbrück and over the river, her cousin, Martin, sits beside her in the front seat staring out the window. It's been a long emotional day and he looks tired. When we turn north toward Seefeld, I can see that his eyelids are heavy. By the time we reach the German border near Mittenwald, he's sound asleep.

Settled into the back seat with Basti and me, *Uroma* Anna seems unsettled and she begins to talk in a sad, whispery voice. My German still isn't good enough to understand everything, but the bits I pick up are enough to make me realize that she is proud of her sister but not so much of herself. I lock eyes with Basti and can almost feel his pain. I don't want her to confess anything that would make me like her less and I can only imagine how it would devastate Basti. As she pours out her story, I escape into sleep.

****

When I open my eyes again, I notice that *Uroma* Anna is sleeping and Basti looks destroyed. I touch his arm and ask, "Are you okay?"

"I've had better days."

"Would it help to talk about it, Basti?"

He nods and then says. "*Uroma* was talking about the war days and how people reacted for good or for evil. Fear almost consumed them in those days but, in the end, she said only Liesi had shown courage. She said that today stirred up many memories and she feels more than ever that she didn't do enough back then. I reminded her that she was very young."

"Wasn't she a teenager by the time the Nazis took over?"

"Yes, but what you don't understand is that the bad times in Germany started when she was a small child, only three years old."

"You're right, Basti; I don't understand. What happened then?"

"Germany lost World War I and the people felt shame. Also, they had little food and supplies. That was when many

Germans began listening to Adolph Hitler. He argued that Germany lost the war because of Jews and Bolsheviks."

"But that wasn't true! Did many people believe him?"

"Some. She said that her parents didn't trust Hitler's motives when he and his friends tried to topple the government in 1923 but even at 8 years old, she was smart enough to sense that criticism of him was dangerous. Just a year later, when Hitler put his views into a book called *Mein Kampf*, more and more of her family's friends paid attention to him."

"Why?"

"Inflation got so bad that many people couldn't afford to feed their families and heat their homes. Even her own parents stood on breadlines and gathered sticks to burn."

"Okay, but did *she* pay attention to him?"

"She said it eventually became hard not to and that it's hard to explain now because things were so different… so confusing… so overwhelming."

"For example?"

"When she was about thirteen, the Hitler Youth movement started and her friends were all joining. She didn't want to be a social outcast so she also joined. Her parents weren't happy about it, but they didn't stop her."

"I don't know… maybe I'm unusual but I've never been one to follow the crowd, especially if I thought they were wrong." When I see the hurt look on Basti's face, I realize I sound smug. "Basti, I'm not judging your *Uroma*. It's just hard to understand what it was like back then. Did she actually like being in the Hitler Youth?"

"She said it was fun for a while, but certain things began to bother her. The group was always pushing Nazi ideas that seemed at odds with her logical mind and compassionate nature. She was also concerned for her friend Erna who had not been allowed to join because the medical entry exam detected some Jewish blood in her background."

"That's definitely a reason to quit!"

"You need to understand, Ellen Troy, that it was scary to quit. The Nazis could make life miserable for you. Instead, she suggested to her friends that they form their own club so Erna could take part. When they refused and pressured her to stay away from the 'mixed blood,' she was horrified but also frightened. She remained in the group but also remained a friend to Erna. To her everlasting shame though, she kept that friendship a secret from that time on."

"What year was that?"

"1927."

"Yikes! Hitler and the Nazis were barely getting started! It must have gotten worse for her."

"Yes, because kids were expected to follow the Nazi program. If you didn't, you were in big trouble. When she was fifteen, she was switched over to a new group — the

League of German Maidens. She hated this even more. Its main focus was on housekeeping and raising perfect Aryan Nazi children. She loved children and hoped to have some of her own someday but not for the Nazi cause. Besides, she was a good student and wanted to become a doctor."

"Fifteen! I'm fifteen and I can't imagine the government pushing me to have children! That should be a private decision and, for me, it will come way after high school and university and, well, a lot of things! A smart girl like your *Uroma* Anna must have been horrified!"

"She was but she was afraid to say so, even to her friends. Many of them thought that all of the marching and singing, propaganda and pageantry were exciting. Their childhoods had been so dismal with the war and rationing and now... Hitler seemed exciting. Others said that the Nazis were restoring rights to 'real' Germans and so what if the 'riff-raff' was eliminated! In her heart, she didn't believe that Jews, political dissenters and the disabled were not real Germans, much less 'riff-raff,' but for self-preservation she remained a member of the League of German Maidens."

"Basti, she became a doctor so she must have stopped following the program at some point, right?"

"Yes but, at first, her only rebellion was that she missed meetings by pleading schoolwork demands. It wasn't until she was eighteen and studying hard for her *Abitur*, the certificate needed for a university placement, that she had the courage to quit. In order to enter the medical program, she needed a very high score and that left no time for anything else — or so she told her friends. It was risky because it was 1933 and Hitler had become Chancellor of Germany."

"Good for her. Bravery must have paid off because she did go to medical school then, right?"

"Not right away because Hitler and the Nazis didn't make it easy. They required two years of service to the state first. It wasn't until 1936 that she began her medical studies."

"Well, she must have felt good about finally being at the university, right?"

"She said that even the university was scary because some students and staff were Nazis."

"But I thought that universities were places where the brightest minds existed! How could smart people buy into Hitler's craziness? And how could doctors become Nazis? They're supposed to 'do no harm'! That makes me want to vomit!"

"The Nazis took over the whole education system in 1937, Ellen Troy, so brilliant professors who didn't agree risked dismissal, imprisonment and death. As for the doctors, Ellen Troy, theirs is one of the most shameful tales in German history and *Uroma* shudders when she thinks back to those times. Too many doctors seemed to have no conscience."

"Did she tell you what it was like?"

"A little bit. When she received her medical degree in 1941 and began working at one of the large hospitals in *München*, she said she soon realized that the doctors with power were Nazis. She tried to do her job while keeping a low profile and not getting into political discussions. She learned to keep her hands busy with a patient when she spotted a higher-up coming in her direction. That way, when greeted with *'Heil Hitler,'* she could avoid the salute, even if she had to say the words. She tried to focus on medicine and healing but it became increasingly hard to ignore orders that said not to treat racially undesirable patients."

"What did she do, Basti?"

He looks at me with troubled eyes and hesitates. I feel my heart contract but whisper, "Tell me only if you want to."

He looks away for a few seconds and then heaves his shoulders and makes a decision. "I think you've earned the right to know more of my family history, Ellen Troy. She said that she obeyed these rules because she was never sure who might report her. If they did, she could have faced arrest, if not torture, imprisonment, or even death. She told herself that it was the lives of those she *could* help that counted but, more and more, she said that she didn't like herself."

"She must have felt all alone."

"She did until she met my great grandfather, *Doktor* Karsten Schumann. They both were relieved to find out that they agreed about the harm being done in the name of the Nazis. Gruesome medical experiments reported in the German medical journals and rumors of the killing of children with Down's syndrome and other so-called 'abnormalities' disturbed them both. They were afraid to speak out in opposition but they found some release in speaking to each other. They became fast friends, fell in love, and helped one another get through the nightmare with small methods of passive resistance."

"What do you mean?"

"I mean that they tried to do things that weren't obvious like losing paperwork or casting a blind eye when they guessed that a much braver colleague was doing resistance work."

"Well, that was better than nothing, right?"

"*Uroma* said that it was a feeble effort. It haunts her, along with fragments of awful scenarios that she remembers — a severely bleeding man dragged out of the emergency room by the Gestapo, a handicapped young woman being transferred to a clinic for involuntary sterilization, and worst of all for her personally, the 'evacuation' of her old friend Erna to the East, never to be heard from again."

When Basti stops talking, he looks the way I feel — wrecked. His beloved *Uroma* Anna has given him a very personal confession of things she *didn't* do. I want to tell him it's not that bad but I can't. Her story makes me realize that evil doesn't just need active helpers for it to grow. Good people frozen by fear into inaction also make it possible. A chill runs through me.

Basti has tears running down his cheeks and I'm at a loss for how to comfort him. What can you say about a loved one's admitted lack of bravery? Does a good life make up for it?

With tears in my own eyes, I ask him, "Are you okay?"

He looks a bit shaky but he nods and says, "Thank you for listening, Ellen Troy."

The only response I can manage is a hug.

For the rest of the ride, I wonder how brave I would have been under those circumstances. What if similar things happened now? I've always taken for granted the fact that I'm welcome in the foreign countries I've lived, but what if I was targeted for being American? Or imprisoned because I have psychic dreams? Worse yet, what if I was threatened with death for being Basti's friend? How brave would I be? Then it occurs to me that similar things do happen today in many countries, even my own. I think of kids I've read about in the States who have died because they refused to join a teenage gang. The Nazis were a gang of gigantic magnitude that targeted all ages. These thoughts give me the shivers and I hope I never have to be tested that way.

As we get close to home, *Uroma* Anna opens her eyes. Looking at Basti, she says that she wishes she could tell him something to make him proud of her. He tells her that he's proud that she had helped some people in small ways.

"Nicht genug." "Not enough," is her answer.

Chapter 36 — *Auf Wieder Sehen*

It's Saturday, the day of our departure. I hear Mom's voice call, reminding me that we have to leave for the airport by 8 am but I take time to make a final note about Basti's family in my diary. I add that the Königs adopted Christoph and I'm about to write down the name of Liesi's husband but I stop myself. Magda and the Königs had refused to put his name on her gravestone so I leave him nameless as well.

Christoph and Sigrid Falke
great, great grandparents (built Haus Falke)

Dr. Anna (Falke) Schumann   *Elizabeth (Liesi) Falke*
great grandma (Uroma)   *(Gisela von Werz) (m..)*
                                    (died 1946)

Dr. Sabine Müller   *Christoph König*
Grandma (Oma)   *(adopted by Königs)*
                                  (son-died 2008)

Silke Hofstetter (m. Franz)   *Lukas König (grandson)*
Parents

Sebastian (Basti) & Annika

When that is done, I look around my barren bedroom from which most of my personal things have been removed. They're already on the way to our next destination. It looks the way I remember seeing it for the first time, a little more than a year ago. The simple wooden bed is positioned next to the window. The freestanding wooden *Schrank* stands against the opposite wall and it occurs to me that I have never referred to it as a closet or wardrobe here, even when speaking English. It has distinctive carving on the doors and replaces the non-existent built-in closets in German homes. It's one of those things that will always retain its German name for me. I find that each of Dad's assignments leave pieces of the host country language imbedded in my brain in various ways. It's like our Italian phone number. I will always remember it in Italian *(otto-sei-sette-otto-tre-otto-due)* and then translate it into English in my head.

It's only 6:30 am but I need time to dress and to say good-bye to Basti. Neither of us said goodbye last night when we returned from Innsbrück. I couldn't bear to say the words and I sensed that he couldn't either. He said only that he would see me in the morning.

Downstairs, the suitcases are piled in the front hall and the sight of them depresses me. I step past them and make my way into the kitchen where Mom and Dad are having coffee and T.G. is eating breakfast as if it's his last meal — at least that hasn't changed. I slide into a chair at the table and take a sip of juice but I have no appetite and no inclination to participate in conversation. I'm pretty much tuning everyone out until I hear Dad say "Hofstetter." He's ready to go next door to return the key and he suggests that we all go along to say good-bye to our friends and thank them for their kindnesses during our stay. Of course it's the right thing to do but I'm somehow disappointed. I had hoped to have some time alone with Basti but I gather my things and lug them outside. It's hard to watch Dad lock the front door of *Haus* Falke for the final time.

When the car is packed and ready, we all head next door. Before we can ring the bell, *Herr* Hofstetter pulls it open and welcomes us to enter. *Uroma* Anna, *Frau* Silke and Annika aren't far behind and *Frau* Silke insists that we take the time for another *Kaffee* since *Oma* Sabine is busy brewing it as we speak. She herds our family toward the kitchen but pulls me aside. With a conspiratorial smile she whispers, *"Basti ist im Garten."*

I thank her and head outside. He's sitting cross-legged and looking somber under the shade tree but he smiles when he sees me and I run to sit beside him.

After an awkward silence, I lift the locket and chain up and over my head and offer it to him. "You should have this, Basti. Other than her bones, it's the only part of Liesi that's left."

He looks at the antique locket and accepts it without speaking. He reaches into his pocket, takes out a photo and a small pair of scissors, pries open the locket, removes Magda's photo, and then places it over the new photo as a template. He cuts it to size and then inserts the new one over the old one.

At first he hesitates but then looks into my eyes. "You have a special bond with her now Ellen Troy and I think she would like you to wear the locket. I hope that she'd approve of you having my picture now. I know that I want you to have it. That way, perhaps you won't forget me."

I'm speechless and tears start to flow. Basti gestures as if to put the locket back over my head and I nod. He places it back, kisses my cheek and whispers, "You are special, Ellen Troy."

The tender moment is interrupted by T.G. yelling that it's time to go. I'm annoyed but yet also grateful. How can I possibly tell Basti how I really feel, how special he is too?

I hop to my feet, say that I should say good-bye to the others, and start walking away. Suddenly, I stop. I walk back with determination and kiss him. Before the startled boy can react, I pull away and begin running toward the back door.

"Write to me Ellen Troy!"

I want to yell back that I will write lots and lots but I'm crying too much. I'm on my way to my native land, to a very small town in the state of Maine. It's a very long way from Basti and I think that my heart might break.

Chapter 37 — The Following June

The school term in Maine has finished and I'm finally on my way to Samnaun, Switzerland. The group assembling at Sankt Jacob's will come from far and wide but they will all be there for closure of one sort or another.

Frau Doktor Anna Falke Schumann will come from Munich, Germany, accompanied by *Oma* Sabine, Silke, Franz, Basti and Annika. It's not their first visit but it will be a momentous one. *Uroma* Anna has arranged for a new headstone for her sister. It includes both Liesi's given name and her Resistance name.

Elisabeth Beatrix Falke
Widerstandname: Gisela von Werz
1920–1946

Petra and Lukas König will accompany Christoph's remains from Innsbrück, Austria. After much thought, they decided that he belongs next to his birth mother and near the Königs, the adoptive parents who loved him. His simple flat stone will rest to the left of Liesi's.

Doctor Martin Grüber will accompany John MacDougal from California, U.S.A. When the doctor returned to the States last September, Mr. MacDougal was eager to hear what happened. He was moved by the developments in the story that his "Ute" was part of. When this day's arrangements were conceived, Mr. MacDougal told Doctor Martin that he believed that "Ute" would have wanted him to be there. In fact, he had saved some of her ashes in hopes of returning them to her native land. However, after learning of her brave efforts, he decided it was fitting that they be buried in Switzerland near her friend and fellow resistance worker, "Gisela." It was at this point that Doctor Martin realized that he needed to betray part of his promise to Magda. He told John MacDougal of the name change and her reasons for keeping it from him. Mr. MacDougal was shocked but held no grudge. If anything, it made his wife's exploits all the more daring and admirable.

So, John MacDougal will be by Doctor Martin's side today and Magda's flat stone will flank the right side of Liesi's grave. The inscription might seem a bit odd to her husband.

Magdalena Gudrun Alt MacDougal
Widerstandname: Ute Seidl
1920–2014

The rest of the group will come out of friendship, love, and support and to pay their respects. This will include *Doktor* Erika Grüber and her parents, all four members of the Van Hoorn family and Liesi's old sweetheart, Helmar Fürstenrieder.

As our Audi rental nears Samnaun, Mom and I hear the church bells begin to ring in preparation for the memorial service. My stomach is in knots because so much has happened this past year without Basti. I haven't forgotten him but I haven't been the best communicator either. Will he be angry? Or worse, will he not care? Relief floods over me when our eyes meet, and I realize that he seems happy to see me.

Mom and I arrive just in time. A procession of priests is emerging from the church and Basti and I have no time for small talk. Like everyone else, we focus on the reasons we are here. A priest offers up prayers for the departed, sprinkles incense over their graves, and the family (for we are all one family in spirit) gives back with prayerful responses. When the last *Amen* is said, the priest beckons Doctor Martin to step forward to give the eulogy for the two women. He appears less stressed than last year as he reads the German words with an American accent. Afterward, his strong voice rings out with the English translation.

"The Liesis and Magdas of the Nazi world my papa once lived in were far too scarce, almost non-existent in fact and that has been Germany's shameful legacy in the eyes of the world. Just think how different that time might have been if more individuals had questioned and acted out against the Nazis.

"You might think that they were different from most people, that they weren't scared, but that wasn't true. It was a horrific time, and they were as frightened as anybody.

"You might think that they had a better opportunity to make a difference since they were in the medical profession but that wasn't true either. The authorities were asking German physicians at that time to validate 'racial hygiene' with medical proof. They were watched closely with suspicion and far too many lacked the moral courage to resist.

"On the other hand, you might think that they didn't do enough. They worked only to save German children, while the Jews and Gypsies, handicapped and mentally ill, and so many others still kept going to the ovens and the camps. Yes, what they did was only a small band-aid on the abscess of Nazi evil but it kept the toxic pus from oozing out faster. It may not have been enough but it was something.

"They were both just in their early twenties when they risked their lives and I find that remarkable when the masses of those who were older and should have been wiser took the head-in-the-sand approach and did nothing.

"These two young women were just individual human beings who did what they thought was right and my papa was proud to know them."

He steps back and the priest then nods to Lukas who comes forward to give the eulogy for his papa, first in German and then in English. Lukas is *still* impressive!

"My papa was not perfect but he taught me some good things. He was a victim of the war in many ways and he unfortunately never got to know his mother, who would have been a good influence. Luckily, two other good people raised him and tried to pass on their values. Like many teenagers, however, he didn't listen and his life became hard. Their influence must have always been at the back of his brain somewhere, however. When it counted for me, he did listen and show that he cared. He taught me that people can change for the better, even after a long time, if they let themselves be open to good ideas from good people. I never met *Herr* Johann König and his wife Helga but I would like to thank them for loving my papa. Because of them, he was able to love me. I wish that my papa hadn't died but I'm glad he is here with his two mamas and his best papa."

Lukas then takes three white roses and lays one upon each grave. His papa's stone is the last and it too has a new inscription.

Christoph Lukas Falke König
1946–2008

The silence is broken by the fluttering sound of wings and I sense the crow before I see it. It's resting on Liesi's headstone — only it isn't a crow, it's a white dove! I watch as it stretches its wings, looks my way, and then takes off into the sky disappearing from view. No one else seems to have noticed but then my eyes lock with Basti's and I know that he saw it too and understands.

As the ceremony concludes and people start to leave, Basti and I walk closer to the graves for a quiet moment alone with the people we found. I'm not sure what he's thinking but my mind is drawn back to my final days learning the details of their lives. It was so hectic and there was no time for me to give much thought to my next destination.

As if reading my thoughts, Basti whispers, "So, Ellen Troy, did you find out amazing things in America too?" I smile at Basti and nod. "Let's just say that staying with my grandparents wasn't boring and my psychic ability works even in the Maine woods."

Afterword

The brave main German characters in this story, *Doktor* Heribert Grüber, Elizabeth (Liesi) Falke, and Magdalena (Magda) Alt are fictional. However, the members of The White Rose who distributed the anti-Nazi leaflets were real people. The White Rose was formed in 1941 by a group from the University of Munich. Hans Scholl, Christoph Probst, Alexander Schmorell, and Willi Graf were all medical students. Professor Kurt Huber was a philosophy professor and Sophie Scholl was a biology and philosophy student. They were all arrested by the Nazis and beheaded by guillotine in 1943.

Hans Leipelt, a chemistry student and White Rose member was beheaded in 1945 for reproducing and distributing the sixth and final White Rose leaflet in Hamburg and for collecting money to help Professor Huber's widow. Another medical student and member of the White Rose, Jürgen (George) Wittenstein, was interrogated by the Gestapo but they couldn't prove his involvement so they let him go. He got himself transferred to the Italian front beyond Nazi control and smuggled weapons back to Munich for another resistance group. He was the only one of the White Rose to survive. After the war, he relocated to the United States and became a doctor. Others participated by funding the efforts, providing supplies and tools, and distributing the leaflets.

Book Suggestions:

If you are interested in reading more about The White Rose: Scholl, Inge. <u>The White Rose: Munich 1942-1943</u>. Translated from German by Arthur R. Schultz. (1983). Middletown, CT: Wesleyan University Press.

****

If you enjoyed *White Flutters in Munich*, be sure to check out my first book in the E.T. Madigan series of mysteries:

<u>**Upheavals at Cuma**</u>

Twelve-year-old Ellen Theodora Madigan doesn't want to be a psychic. However, when her family moves to Cuma, Italy and lands her at the site of one of the renowned ancient oracles — the Cumaean Sibyl, she no longer has a choice. Her supernatural gift brings on strange dreams and the feeling that an old mystery on the Cuma hillside needs to be solved.

Ellen's curiosity is heightened by a series of disturbing events that all seem to be connected to a pet collar she obtains from a local farmer. While coming to terms with her paranormal gift, she is confronted with cryptic messages, attempted murder and sybilline ghosts and must use her wits to solve two mysterious long-ago deaths. In the process, she must convince her family, her newfound Italian friends and even NATO to help her set things in motion. Good thing, because these deaths have international repercussions!

Thanks for reading,
Joan Wright Mularz

07/16

Atlanta-Fulton Public Library